QUADRILLE

QUADRILLE

Marion Chesney

Chivers Press
Bath, England

•

Thorndike Press
Waterville, Maine USA

This Large Print edition is published by Chivers Press, England, and by Thorndike Press, USA.

Published in 2002 in the U.K. by arrangement with the author.

Published in 2002 in the U.S. by arrangement with Lowenstein Associates, Inc.

U.K. Hardcover ISBN 0–7540–4708–3   (Chivers Large Print)
U.K. Softcover   ISBN 0–7540–4709–1   (Camden Large Print)
U.S. Softcover   ISBN 0–7862–3668–X (General Series Edition)

The text of this Large Print edition is unabridged.
Other aspects of the book may vary from the original edition.

Set in 16 pt. New Times Roman.

Printed in Great Britain on acid-free paper.

British Library Cataloguing in Publication Data available

Library of Congress Cataloging-in-Publication Data

Chesney, Marion.
      Quadrille / Marion Chesney.
            p.   cm.
      ISBN 0–7862–3668–X (lg. print : sc : alk. paper)
      1. Large type books. I. Title.
   PR6053.H4535 Q33 2002
   823'.914—dc21   2001043395

*For Eileen and Tom Kerr
with love*

CHAPTER ONE

'I do not want to go to Clarissa's,' said Lady Mary Challenge, standing beside the open window to try to catch a breath of cool air.

'You will do as you are told, madam,' said her husband, Colonel, Lord Hubert Challenge, from his position in front of the looking glass.

Mary stifled a little sigh. So it had begun and so it would go on in this loveless marriage. He issued the commands, she must obey. She turned and surveyed her husband who was shrugging his muscular shoulders into his evening jacket. The room was lit by one branch of candles on the mantelpiece and his reflection looked almost satanic in their wavering light. It was a handsome if swarthy face with a strong chin and a firm mouth. He had a patrician nose and large, beautiful brown eyes, very well spaced and ornamented with long thick lashes which detracted not one whit from his overpowering air of masculinity. His thick black hair sprung in two wings from his high forehead and his tall figure moved with athletic grace as he turned to face her.

Mary turned away. She did not want to read the expression in his eyes, for she knew she looked dowdy. Her dress of heavy silk was overfussy, giving her immature figure an awkward air. She had a smooth madonna-like

1

face with an almost translucent skin and two large gray eyes and a quantity of fine, light, brown hair but it was her shy cringing air which made her appear dowdy, rather than her unfashionable clothes.

'I told you before that Lady Clarissa is an old friend of mine,' said Lord Hubert, turning away from her and searching through the card rack for the correct invitation.

'All Brussels knows of your friendship with Clarissa,' thought Mary, but she did not have the courage to say it aloud.

Mary knew herself to be a wealthy heiress. She knew also that Lord Hubert had married her for her money in order to save his ancestral home. Mary had naively expected love to blossom in this arranged marriage. But no sooner was she his wife than, three weeks after they were married, his regiment was ordered to Brussels.

He hadn't wanted her to go with him but she had insisted with a pertinacity foreign to her shy nature and he had shrugged and agreed. She had fondly imagined a grim battlefront—for wasn't that ogre Napoleon back to ravage Europe?—where she would have her husband all to herself.

But never in her wildest dreams had she imagined the sophisticated, glittering scene that was Brussels, where every society beauty seemed to be gathered to dazzle and charm her susceptible husband. And Clarissa, Lady

Thorbury, was the most beautiful of all. Already Mary had heard it rumored that Clarissa had been her husband's mistress before their marriage and before her subsequent engagement to Viscount Peregrine St. James.

'There are rumors that Napoleon's troops are at Quatre Bras,' ventured Mary timidly to try to turn the conversation away from Lady Clarissa.

'Gossiping women,' said Lord Hubert impatiently. 'What do they know of military matters?'

Mary opened her mouth to point out that it was the elderly Colonel Chalmers who had given her the news but her husband had already marched to the door and was holding it open.

She bent her head and walked before him down the stone steps from their rented apartment and out into the warm June night. The streets were thronged with carriages, their lamps gleaming and flashing in the dark blue night. Ladies laughed and flirted their fans and the officers escorting them seemed as merry as ever. But the undertone everywhere was war. War stalked the cobbled streets and brooded in the darkness of the Park. The laughter had an edge and faces were lit with a hectic look.

Lady Mary was suddenly afraid for her husband. She wanted to talk to him about the forthcoming battle. At first it had seemed

3

during the past carefree sunny days that Napoleon was merely some type of low criminal who would soon be fettered and chained by the might of the allied armies. But frightened rumors and scared whispers had grown in volume. Every time she had tried to convey her fears to her husband he had snapped back that she knew nothing of such things, and so she had to hug her fear to herself. She was too timid and retiring and countrified to make any friends among the dashing Brussels belles and so she had no one to confide in.

'Not that I ever had anyone to confide in,' thought Mary bitterly. Her parents, two grim members of the untitled aristocracy, had passed her over to the care of a nurse and then a governess since that day she had surprised them by coming into the world when her mother was forty-eight and her father fifty.

When she reached her seventeenth birthday, they had seemed to notice her for the first time. 'Why, Mary, you have become a woman,' her mother, Mrs. Tyre, had said with a grim smile. The next week she was affianced, whether she liked it or not, to the impecunious Lord Challenge, the Tyres having decided it was time they had a title in the family.

Mary had fallen desperately in love with Lord Hubert with all the aching, tremulous passion of first love. But on their wedding night, he had brutally told her that he did not seduce virgins. It was an arranged marriage, nothing more. He would not interfere with her, provided she left him alone.

But still she had hoped. Until the day they had arrived in Brussels and Lady Clarissa had appeared as their first guest, looking at Lord Hubert with melting eyes. Every line of her body could be seen plainly through a transparent muslin gown, hinting at all sorts of untold intimacies.

Damn Clarissa! Mary's eyes filled with unshed tears. The carriage rolled to a halt and Mary braced herself for the ordeal.

At first she thought it was not going to be as bad as she had feared. Clarissa welcomed them, hanging onto the arm of her fiancé, Lord Peregrine. Lord Peregrine was a thickset, brutish man with a fat, blue chin and a great hooked nose. He had small twinkling eyes and his face was always creased up in a jolly laugh; but nothing could disguise the atmosphere of suppressed rage that he seemed to carry about with him. Mary did not like him one bit. But he was Clarissa's fiancé and therefore his presence surely meant that Clarissa would be too occupied to flirt with Lord Hubert.

Clarissa was a buxom redhead of about thirty years. Her dress of gold tissue was damped to cling to her body and Mary could not help hoping she caught a fatal chill. Clarissa had green eyes which were strangely narrow and slightly tilted. They were of a pale green color and gave her appearance the lazy sensuality of a cat.

The company chattered of everything but war, and Mary wondered why they did not seem to feel its brooding presence creeping in from the streets.

Apart from Clarissa and Lord Peregrine, Mary and Lord Hubert, there were two other couples present.

There was a Major Frederick Godwin and his wife, Lucy. Major Godwin was a big, slow-speaking man, handsome in a florid way. He had thick, fair hair and a fine pair of military sideburns. His wife Lucy was small, pretty, vivacious and cruel. Her husband stared at her in dumb adoration while she pouted and flirted with all the men present. She had curly blonde hair confined over one ear with a blue silk ribbon and a ball gown of celestial blue muslin which enhanced the Dresden china perfection of her features.

The other couple struck Mary as being a very odd pair to find in high society. Their names were Mr. and Mrs. Witherspoon and they were hearty, jolly, middle-aged and very vulgar. They "my lorded" and "my ladied" all the titles to death, and when they weren't doing that they were claiming friendship with every notable in Brussels, from the Duke of Wellington to the Prince of Orange.

Mrs. Witherspoon patted her hideous turban complacently and turned her full

6

attention on Lord Hubert. 'Was you going to open up your town house in London?' she asked.

'If I come out of this affair alive,' he said coldly.

'Such a fine house it is too,' said Mrs. Witherspoon, laying a fat white hand on his jacket sleeve. 'Such a pity it had to be kept closed all these years. St. James's Square, it is, I believe. It's a wonder you didn't sell it when you was so down in funds.'

There was a startled silence, and then Lord Hubert looked down at the hand on his jacket as if some white slug were crawling up his arm.

'You seem to be well versed in my affairs, madam,' he remarked, turning away.

'Oh, ain't I just,' crowed Mrs. Witherspoon, peering round to see his averted face. 'I know all about you, my lord. I remember when it was rumored that Hammonds, your pa's old home, was to go under the hammer. What a pity, I said to Mr. Witherspoon, for it breaks my heart to see an old home going out of the family. "Never fear, my love," says he, "for that young spark'll find the money even if he has to marry to get it."'

There was an appalled silence which penetrated even Mrs. Witherspoon's thick hide, for she added hurriedly, 'It was just his little joke for I can see by looking at you and your lovely wife, my lord, that if ever I did see a pair of lovebirds . . .'

7

'Madam, pray keep your distasteful and vulgar observations to yourself,' said Lord Hubert.

'That's right, my lord,' remarked Mrs. Witherspoon complacently, 'as I was saying to the dear Dook only yesterday, I says, "Arthur," I says, "I likes a gentleman who can take a joke."'

'Come Mrs. Witherspoon,' said Lady Clarissa hurriedly, 'you are not eating your food.'

'We're newly married ourselves,' said Major Godwin with a fond smile at his wife, Lucy, who pouted and stared at the table.

'Why must you tell everyone we're just married?' complained Lucy.

'Because it's true, my love,' said Major Godwin in surprise.

'Oh, you're such a *dull* old stick, Freddie,' said his wife with a brittle laugh.

There was another embarrassed silence and Mary racked her brains for something to say.

'Your little wife is very quiet,' said Clarissa to Lord Hubert. 'I do believe you beat her.'

'Do you think this affair at Quatre Bras will come to anything?' Lord Hubert asked Major Freddie Godwin.

'Can't say till we join the chaps in the morning and see for ourselves,' said Freddie.

Clarissa frowned and bit her lip. Hubert was not going to let her attack his little wife in any way. Why had he married that countrified nobody anyway? *She* could have given him money. And hadn't he been her lover for two delirious years before this strange marriage? Now Hubert was stuck with a wife he obviously did not want, and she had gone and got herself engaged to Perry in a fit of pique at the news of Hubert's wedding.

Well, she would punish him. Somehow, she would have him back in her arms. She became aware that Mr. Witherspoon was addressing her.

'My lady,' said that gentleman, 'my good wife informs me that a young officer has just ridden up to your front door looking all of a lather.' He paused and looked at Clarissa expectantly.

'*I*,' said Clarissa sweetly, 'have servants to answer the door for me.'

'But I wonder . . .' began the unsnubbable Mr. Witherspoon. But at that moment a servant entered, and said that Captain Harry Black was anxious to have a word with Lord Challenge.

Lord Challenge left the room with the curious eyes of the Witherspoons boring into his back. Clarissa called the servant back. 'Tell Captain Black to join us for a glass of wine.'

The servant bowed and withdrew. A thin, nervous young Captain walked into the room carrying a portfolio which he clutched tightly under one arm, followed by Lord Hubert.

'Harry,' smiled Clarissa, 'how divine to see

you again.'

'Not another,' said her fiancé, Lord Peregrine, with a heavy sneer, and Captain Black blushed. 'I really must go,' he said, but Clarissa stood up and wound her white arms around his neck. 'We are just moving to the drawing room, dear Captain,' she cooed. 'Do put down that silly portfolio and come and join us.'

'I am not supposed to let it out of my sight,' said Captain Black. 'I . . .'

'Oh, *silly*,' laughed Clarissa. 'Which one of us here is going to steal it?'

'I didn't mean that, my lady. I meant . . .' But Clarissa was already leading him out of the door after having taken the portfolio from under his arm and dropped it carelessly onto the table.

Mary looked sympathetically towards Lord Peregrine. She did not like him, but she could not help feeling sorry for him as he stood by the empty fireplace, scowling furiously at the hearth.

She looked round for her husband but Lucy Godwin was talking to him in a very animated fashion. Lord Hubert was smiling down into her eyes in a way that he certainly never showed to poor Mary.

She gave a tiny sigh and turned as she heard a small echo of it behind her. Major Freddie Godwin was standing miserably behind her, fingering his sideburns and watching his wife.

10

'Do I look like that?' thought Mary suddenly. 'Hurt and lost and oh! so transparent?'

'Come, Captain Godwin,' she said with a boldness that amazed her, 'you shall escort me to the drawing room. Tell me, do you think we shall still be going on to the ball?'

'Oh, I think so,' said the Major, reluctantly tearing his eyes away from his wife and offering Mary his arm. 'We've orders to march in the morning, but Wellington's to be at the ball so we may as well be there too.'

'Does Hubert march, too?' asked Mary faintly.

'Dash it, didn't he tell you? He's bound to, you know. His regiment's out there already.'

He led her into the drawing room and sat next to her on a small sofa.

Ignoring Mary's obvious distress, the Major took her gloved hands in his and looked earnestly into her eyes.

'I say, Lady Challenge, do you think you could keep an eye on little Lucy for me while I'm away? She's just a child, you know. So beautiful and, well,' here the poor Major tugged desperately at his sideburns, 'if something happens to me I'd like to think that she's in capable hands.'

For all her distress, Mary could not help reflecting bitterly that she, Mary, was seventeen and the beautiful Lucy a mature twenty. But beauty, she thought sadly, is

11

always considered vulnerable.

'What are our chances of victory?' she asked in a low voice.

'Oh, we'll win,' said the large Major cheerfully. 'Napoleon's nothing compared to our Duke. Why, look how Wellington routed them in the Peninsula!' But his eyes held a worried look.

'But *why*,' said Mary intensely, '*why* must we all go to this ball? It is eleven o'clock in the evening and if you must march in the morning, surely you at least want to spend some time alone with your wife?'

'Well, I would and that's a fact,' he said miserably. 'But Lucy was so thrilled to get the Duchess of Richmond's invitation that she would go even if Napoleon himself, and all his troops, were to be there.

'Fact is,' he said with a sudden burst of confidence, 'I feel Lucy's had rather a hard time of it. We were neighbors, you know, and she had never really met any other fellows when she married me. I've got the family place in London and the minute we were married I decided to give her a Season. She got a great deal of attention for she is so very beautiful, you know, and she sometimes feels that perhaps she could have done better than have married a stick-in-the-mud like me.'

'She surely did not say so!' exclaimed Mary, shocked.

'No,' lied the gallant Major, 'but I love her

12

and I notice things.'

Mary was overcome by a rush of affection for the miserable Major. After all, who knew better than herself what it was like to be married to someone one adored, and to receive no love in return?

'I shall take care of her,' she said in a quiet voice, squeezing the Major's large hands sympathetically in her own, and smiling up into his eyes.

She then looked across the room and caught the faintly surprised look on her husband's face and the hard, china blue stare of Lucy.

At that moment, the Captain took his leave and Clarissa announced gaily that they should leave for the ball.

Once more into the warm night they went, with the Witherspoons clinging like limpets.

'Surely *they* are not invited to the Richmonds?' said Lord Hubert as they stood on the street outside waiting for their carriages. 'Where did you find such pushing mushrooms, Clarissa?'

But Clarissa only laughed and would not reply.

They made their way towards the Duchess of Richmond's house as the drums began to beat and the trumpets sounded, calling the soldiers to arms.

The ballroom was on the ground floor of the Richmond's rented house in the Rue de la Blanchisserie. All the curtains were drawn

13

back, and golden light flooded out onto the cobbles of the street.

All the beauties were there, and all the list of chivalry—ambassadors, generals and aristocrats, and dashing young officers.

Mary felt suddenly weary and wished she could go home to lie down and sleep. She clung to her husband's arm as they entered the ballroom and, wide-eyed, looked round at the magnificence of the tent-like hangings in the royal colors of crimson, gold and black, the rose-trellised wallpaper and the glittering chandeliers.

She made her curtsy to the Duke and Duchess of Richmond, and turned to say something to her husband. But he was staring toward the doorway where a tall figure, glittering with orders, had just entered. The newcomer had a handsome tanned face, close-cropped black hair and a hooked nose. He laughed at something the Duke of Richmond was saying and his laugh echoed round the ballroom in great jerks of sound, like a hyena with the whooping cough. There was no mistaking that laugh or those vivid blue eyes. The Duke of Wellington had arrived.

A seventeen-year-old beauty, Lady Georgiana Lennox, left off dancing and rushed up to the Duke asking whether the rumors of war were true.

Wellington replied gravely, 'Yes, they are true. We are off tomorrow.'

14

'Oh, let us go home,' Mary urged her husband.

'In such a hurry to see me die?' he asked cruelly. He then shook off her arm with some impatience, leaving her to find her own way to a sofa in an embrasure.

The ballroom vibrated with whispers and hurried leave-takings as the officers whose regiments were farthest away slipped quietly from the ballroom. The Duke of Brunswick felt a premonition of death and dropped the little Prince de Ligne off his lap. Wellington sat on a sofa next to Lady Hamilton-Dalrymple, chatting with her and looking very much at his ease, although he kept turning round to whisper orders to various officers who came up to him, one of whom was Lord Hubert.

Clarissa caught hold of Hubert's arm as he was making his way back across the ballroom. 'Hubert,' she breathed huskily. 'When am I to see you alone?'

'Perhaps tonight,' he replied seriously. 'For tonight may be my last.'

'Then spend it with *me*,' she urged, and then reluctantly released his arm as Lord Peregrine came scowling up to them.

Major Godwin detached Lucy from her court of admirers. 'I've got to go now, Lucy. At least I've got one hour before I join my regiment. Come home with me.'

'No,' pouted Lucy. 'Why are you so dramatic? Everyone knows that the dear Duke will defeat Boney. You simply don't want me to have any fun. You may have the next dance with me before you go but that is all.'

'Oh, Lucy,' groaned the Major sadly, but couples were already making up sets for the quadrille.

Hubert strolled towards where his wife was sitting. She looked timid, sad and colorless and he suddenly felt impatient with her. Clarissa had issued an invitation, and he had a good mind to accept it. Mary need never know.

But if he died, he would like to think he had left an heir to inherit Hammonds.

'We leave after this dance, Mary,' he said, looking down at her and holding out his hand. 'Come!'

'Wasn't this a clever idea of mine, my love,' Mr. Witherspoon was saying gleefully to his wife. 'These grand folk who would look down their noses at us at home are all too anxious to be civil when there's a war in the offing.'

Mrs. Maria Witherspoon nodded her turbaned head vigorously. Mr. Witherspoon's fortune hailed from a series of Yorkshire mills. The Witherspoons were therefore 'in trade,' and had found that their vast wealth would not open one society door to them in London. It was then that Mr. Josiah Witherspoon had hit on the idea of going to Brussels.

By being very free with his money and giving various sumptuous banquets in restaurants, he had soon found himself on

16

hobnobbing terms with a variety of titled names who would have cut him dead in Bond Street.

The Witherspoons were an unprepossessing couple, both being on the plump side and a similarity of disposition having marked each face with a permanent ingratiating leer. They had secured invitations to the Duchess of Richmond's ball by simply buying two cards of invitation from a pair of impecunious aristocrats.

But Mrs. Witherspoon's sharp ears had caught a nasty comment earlier that evening. 'My dear,' one lady had said to the other, 'aren't the Witherspoons too simply terrible for words? But after all, one need not recognize them in London.'

She saw Lord Hubert and his wife standing up for the quadrille and noticed that they needed one other couple and accordingly urged her husband into the dance.

The eight members of Lord Hubert's quadrille waited for the opening chords of the music.

'I shall never forget this evening or these dreadful people,' thought Mary, looking round at the other members of the quadrille. 'Apart from Hubert, I never want to see any of them again.'

There were the Witherspoons, simpering awfully and calculating how much social use each member of the quadrille could possibly be to them. There was Lucy, her large eyes roving in every direction but that of her husband. Clarissa was staring at Mary with a hard, calculating look and Lord Peregrine was looking as restless and angry as ever.

The band struck up. The couples bowed and curtsied. They crossed and recrossed, weaving out the patterns of the dance, sometimes dancing with their own partner, sometimes with someone else's.

And the members of Lord Hubert's quadrille did not know that they could at that moment have been acting out a pattern of their lives to come.

* * *

In another room of the Richmond's rented mansion, the Duke of Wellington and the Duke of Richmond were poring over a map.

'Napoleon has *humbugged* me, by God!' said Wellington angrily. 'He has gained twenty-four hours' march on me.'

'What do you intend doing?'

Wellington stared down at the map. 'I have ordered the army to concentrate at Quatre Bras, but we shall not stop him there, and if so,' the Duke passed his thumb-nail over the map, 'I must fight him *here*.'

The Duke of Richmond stared down at the little black name on the map indicated by Wellington's thumbnail.

Waterloo.

CHAPTER TWO

'Why this sudden desire to have me in your bed, my lord?' said Mary wearily.

No reply as her husband unwound his cravat from his neck and shrugged his broad shoulders out of his evening jacket. Hubert had drunk quite a lot of wine that evening. He was tired and he was also excited and elated at the thought of the battle to come.

Mary stood by the window, looking across the shadowed room at his back. She longed to feel his arms around her and at the same time she was alarmed at his air of detachment about the whole thing. He stripped off his shirt and flung it onto a chair where it lay against the dark red plush of the upholstery, gleaming whitely against the darkness of the room.

He turned abruptly and looked at her. He lifted the branch of candles from the mantelpiece and held it high, sending long shadows running and dancing up the walls. Her eyes looked enormous in her white face and she seemed little more than a schoolgirl. He suddenly felt that the correct thing to do would be to deposit a chaste kiss on her forehead and then tuck her into bed. But she was his wife after all and she could really not, in all fairness, expect to remain a virgin for the rest of her life.

He replaced the candelabra on the mantelpiece and walked slowly towards her.

Mary waited, trembling, hanging onto her pride. How dare he flirt with Clarissa one minute and expect her to fall into his arms the next? How dare he shun her for all those long and lonely nights after their marriage? Had he pulled her into his arms as ruthlessly as she expected, then she would have remained still and unresponsive. But instead, he folded his arms gently round her and rocked her against the warmth of his naked chest. 'Come, Mary,' he said softly. 'There is no need to be afraid.'

He tilted her chin and bent his head and kissed her very gently on the mouth, feeling her soft lips cling and tremble against his own. The great love she had for him could no longer be hidden. She gave a little broken sound, half sigh, half sob, and wound her arms round his neck as he lifted her up and carried her to the bed.

Clear and loud below the window came the imperative call of a bugle, and in the nearby squares the drums began to beat to arms. In the back of his brain, he had a nagging feeling of guilt. He should have waited. It was her first night after all and it should not be a hurried affair like this. He should be able to lie at her side late in the morning instead of hurrying off to the battle. But the trembling passion of her immature body against his own suddenly excited him more than anything he could remember before.

He at last fell completely and soundlessly asleep, lying across her body while Mary, cradling him in her arms, dazed with love and happiness, lay awake for a few minutes longer than her lord.

After an hour, a louder bugle call sounded outside and Hubert woke immediately and sat up. Mary awoke as well and stared up at him, eyes almost blind with love. He looked down at her with a strange, abstracted stare. He felt acutely responsible for her for the first time since their marriage and this new feeling of responsibility irked him immensely. And in the same misguided way of parents who are cruel to be kind, he said harshly, 'Dammit, I have overslept!'

Without another look at her, he stalked off to his dressing room, shouting for his valet.

Mary lay, stunned. She felt as if he had slapped her across the face. She could feel the tears pricking at the back of her eyes but she would not let them form. After a few minutes, she got up and wrapped a blanket around herself and crossed to the wash stand in the corner to splash cold water over her face.

She put on a fussy and elaborate pink morning dress, hoping to look her best, but the masses of frills and furbelows only succeeded in making her look younger than ever.

Lord Hubert came into the room, dressed in his scarlet and gold regimentals, looking

21

magnificent, handsome and remote. She stared at him, her eyes wide with hurt, begging for reassurance.

But he avoided her gaze, saying abruptly, 'Should anything happen to me, will you look after Hammonds? It's been in my family for centuries and I would like our son to inherit it . . . if we have a son.'

She nodded dumbly, twisting one of the silly frills of her dress nervously in her fingers.

He crossed the room with easy, athletic strides and called down into the street below for assurance that his horse had been brought round.

'Very well then, Mary,' he said, turning back and dropping a cool kiss on her cheek. 'I must be away. Pray for me.'

'Of course,' said Mary quietly.

He crossed to the door.

'Mary . . .'

'Yes, Hubert?'

'Oh, nothing. Goodbye.' And with that he was gone.

She crossed to the window and leaned out. A rosy dawn was rising over the jumbled gables of Brussels. The air was warm and still and heavy. A flock of pigeons rose and wheeled up to the brightening sky.

A Scotch regiment swung down the street to the skirl of the pipes, then came a regiment of Hussars in their magnificent uniforms.

Then came her husband.

He was sitting on his dappled horse talking to Major Godwin who rode beside him. He seemed to be trying to cheer the Major up. Major Godwin was still in evening dress and dancing pumps, his wife having kept him at the ball until the very last minute.

Hubert suddenly looked up and saw Mary at the window. He raised his arm in a brief salute and rode on.

The regimental band was playing, 'The Girl I Left Behind Me,' a jaunty rousing tune. Mary leaned farther from the window, craning her neck for a last look at her husband, as the remainder of the regiment swung out along the Charleroi road in the rosy glow of the sunrise to join the rest already on the battlefield. She stayed there as all the regiments that had been left in Brussels marched out. She stayed there until the drums and the bugles and the pipes and the marching, marching feet had all filed by and the last fixed bayonet glinted in the sun.

And then she went back into the room to pray.

But Mary was not destined to be allowed to pray in peace. Scarcely had the last military sound disappeared from the streets of Brussels to be replaced by the rumbling of the farm carts arriving for the market than Mrs. Witherspoon was announced.

Mary had not been out in the world enough to recognize a pushing mushroom, or to know what to do about it. Mrs. Witherspoon announced she had come to sit with 'the poor love' and comfort her. Mary did not like Mrs. Witherspoon but she had no one else in Brussels to share her fears with, and so suffered that vulgar lady to stay all morning and then to join her for lunch.

Not that Mrs. Witherspoon seemed very prepared to listen. She had so much to say herself! 'Faith, Lady Mary,' she gushed. 'I feel I have known you this twelvemonth instead of us meeting only the other day. Such a handsome man your husband is and such a rip with the ladies! Ah, now, there's your pretty eyes filling with tears. I do let my tongue rattle on so. Why, the dear Duke—Wellington, you know—was saying only t'other day, "I should have you at the front of the fighting, ma'am. That tongue of yours would put the Frenchies to flight."'

Despite her misery, Mary had to suppress a smile. It did indeed, for once, sound like something the Duke of Wellington might say.

Mrs. Witherspoon continued to eat great quantities of food, seated comfortably in Mary's little dining room, her elbows on the table and a chicken wing in her hand. Her large bosom spilled over the square neckline of a purple silk gown. A purple turban ornamented with an ostrich plume covered her sparse hair, and a stream of non-stop name-dropping issued from her pouting, rosebud

24

mouth as her three chins wiggled vigorously in accompaniment.

Then all of a sudden, Mrs. Witherspoon began to talk about Lord Hubert and Mary learned a great deal about her husband that she did not know before.

Like herself, Lord Hubert had been born when his parents were middle-aged and his mother had not survived the birth. The family fortunes had been dwindling for generations and Hammonds, where Hubert had been brought up, had fallen almost into decay.

His father had died while Hubert was at Oxford; and Hubert had taken what little money there was and had bought himself a captaincy in a regiment which was ordered to Portugal the day he joined it.

He had followed Wellington through Portugal and up the long corridors of Spain to France. At the age of thirty, he had found himself a full colonel with a resounding list of battles behind him: Badajoz, Salamanca and Vittorio to name a few. He had seen more death and bloodshed than he had ever dreamed of. Sometimes in his dreams, he could still hear the screech of the wheels of the bullock carts as they hauled his regiment's provisions across the endless barren sierras. There was the prize money, of course, but every bit of it seemed to be swallowed up in repairs to Hammonds. Wellington forbade looting, and Lord Hubert agreed with this law.

But it was not always easy to impose it when the men seemed hell-bent on looting whole towns and sometimes, seeing brother officers made rich by stolen jewels, wished his conscience would allow him to do the same. At last, in desperation, he began to look about him for a rich wife. Mrs. Witherspoon paused for breath and Mary stared at her, her young face almost hard.

'Tell me, Mrs. Witherspoon,' she said in arctic tones, 'where did you come by such intimate information about my husband? How could you possibly know of his dreams?'

Mrs. Witherspoon bit her lip. She loved gossip and realized she had allowed herself to become carried away. The gossip had mostly come from Lady Clarissa. Even Mrs. Witherspoon, by dint of listening in to everyone else's conversation, had quickly learned that Clarissa had been Lord Hubert's mistress and had wondered along with society why Lord Hubert had not married Clarissa, who was reputed to be mistress of a sizeable fortune.

But the bit about hearing the bullock carts in his dreams she had gleaned from overhearing him talk at a party to one of his brother officers, Peter Bennet. That would do.

'Why, my dear, Lord Hubert told Captain Peter Bennet and that young fellow told me. I don't like to listen to gossip, and that's a fact, but that there Peter was forever talking to me like I was his mother.'

Mary blinked. Peter Bennet was an extremely elegant and fastidious young man. She could not for a minute imagine him confiding in anyone, let alone Mrs. Witherspoon. But she did, however, dismally feel as if the whole of Brussels knew of her husband's innermost thoughts and plans while she, his wife, had only been treated to a few common pleasantries.

The day was hot and hazy and Mary reflected that she had never seen anyone perspire with such unembarrassed abandon as Mrs. Witherspoon. Little rivulets ran down from her forehead, across her chins and joined somewhere at the base of the last chin forming a river which plunged down into the chasm formed by her cleavage. Mary was all at once too tired to school her expression. Open distaste was mirrored in her eyes. Mrs. Witherspoon caught the look as she raised her head from a dish of tansy pudding and her brain began to churn. She would lose this little lady if she did not find some way to make Lady Mary obliged to her.

All at once the hot stillness of the day was broken by a muffled boom.

'What's that!' cried Mary, starting to her feet. 'Thunder?'

Again it sounded and suddenly the street below became alive with the sound of running feet and shouting voices.

Mary leaned out of the window. 'Qui se passe?' she yelled down to the fleeting figures. One Brussels shopkeeper heard her cry and twisted up his head. 'Le feu,' he screamed. 'Le feu, madame! La bataille commence!'

As the sounds of the cannonade boomed even clearer, Mary ran down the stairs and out into the street completely forgetting about Mrs. Witherspoon, and joined the hustling frightened crowd as they streamed towards the Namur Gate to look out across the fields in the direction of Quatre Bras.

All afternoon she stood there, listening in dread to that dull *boom boom boom* which sounded across the heavy air like a death knell. Rumors flew about her. Napoleon had driven a wedge between the British and their allies the Prussians, and he was taking his time to massacre them both. At last, at sunset, the noise of the cannonade died away. Trembling from worry and fatigue, Mary returned to her lodgings.

But she was still not to have her home to herself. Lucy Godwin was waiting for her, her pretty face drawn and pale.

Mary felt a rush of pity for her. 'Do not look *so*, Mrs. Godwin,' she urged. 'Our men will come home victorious, never fear.'

'I'm not worried about Freddie,' said Lucy, hitching a callous shoulder. 'He's used to battles. The thing is—how are we going to escape? Every horse and carriage has been taken and the few seats that are left are going for fabulous sums.'

Mary stared at her amazed. 'But surely you would not contemplate leaving before your husband gets back? How can you dream of leaving, not knowing what has happened to him?'

'I think you're very cold and unfeeling,' pouted Lucy. 'You *promised* Freddie you'd look after me, yes you *did*, for he told me so. And looking after me doesn't mean leaving me here to be raped by a lot of Frenchies.'

'But what can I do? We have no carriage. I have my own horse and, you are welcome to that.'

'I couldn't ride all the way out of here on my own,' protested Lucy. 'It must be a carriage or nothing. Mr. Witherspoon, 'tis said, bought a great deal of horses and at least two carriages apart from his own, and he is selling seats in them at fabulous prices which I cannot afford. *You* are very rich . . .'

'My husband has control of any money we have,' said Mary stiffly. 'I do not inherit any wealth until my parents die.'

'But the Witherspoons are friends of yours . . .'

'I did not set eyes on them until last night.'

'Oh, you're *horrid*,' said Lucy, beginning to sob. 'And so I shall tell Freddie.'

'I shall, however, go and see Mr. Witherspoon,' went on Mary quietly, 'and see

29

what I can do.'

Lucy's tears dried like magic.

The two women had to walk on foot since neither had a carriage and all vehicles of any description had been bought in order to escape the doomed city. The British did not quite realize that the people of Brussels were mostly pro-French and delighted in spreading rumors of Napoleon's successes. The roads from the city were jammed with the carriages of society who had believed up to the very last minute of the ball that Wellington would succeed as he had always done, but no longer had any faith in that great leader.

The Witherspoons had a suite of rooms in the Hotel du Parc. They were delighted to see the ladies, especially Lady Mary. Mrs. Witherspoon and her husband had been plotting all day for some way in which to be of service to young Lady Mary so that they should have subsequent claims on her society in London. As soon as Mary asked for a carriage seat on Lucy's behalf, they brightened considerably. Mr. Witherspoon drooped an eyelid at his wife, which was his signal to tell her to leave things to him. He led Mary into an adjoining room and studied her thoughtfully although the ingratiating leer never left his face. The girl looked exhausted—and vulnerable.

'I shall put it to you plain, my lady,' began Mr. Witherspoon at last. 'I have a seat left in a carriage which is to leave Brussels in an hour's time. Now I will gladly let Mrs. Godwin have it and at no cost whatsoever.'

'You are very kind,' exclaimed Mary, her face lighting up.

'Why, she's quite a little beauty!' thought Mr. Witherspoon. Nonetheless, he pressed on. 'I would like to say I am doing this solely to oblige *you*, Lady Mary, being as how my wife has taken a fancy to you.'

'Too kind,' murmured Mary.

'Now my good wife is very sensitive, very sensitive indeed. Her sensibilities are easily wounded. I would, for example, not like to think that should she wish to call on you in London she would be met with a rebuff.'

Mary was young and immature and unused to the ways of the world. Nonetheless, she knew what was being asked of her and why it was being asked. But she had promised Major Godwin to take care of Lucy.

'I would not dream of rebuffing your wife,' she said gently.

'And I would hope that you would introduce my good Maria to some of the delights of the *ton*? She has no acquaintance in London, you see,' added Mr. Witherspoon, speaking the truth for once.

Mary felt suddenly that should she ever gain safety and feel her husband's arms around her again, she would gladly entertain every pushing Cit in the country.

'Of course. I should be delighted.'

'I hope you don't forget,' said Mr. Witherspoon, his face momentarily losing its habitual leer.

'I am not used to having my word doubted.'

Mr. Witherspoon studied her face for a few seconds and then slowly nodded. 'Best tell Mrs. Lucy to get packed.'

Lucy was ecstatic. She hugged Mary. She even kissed the Witherspoons. She begged Mary to return with her to her lodgings to help her pack.

The sky outside was very black. From overhead came the sinister rumble of thunder. Mary thought dismally of the mud of a water-clogged battlefield and Lucy stared upwards, thinking of all those beautiful roads to freedom which might be washed away.

At last Lucy was packed and seated in the carriage. She looked radiant, flashing smiles at her fellow passengers and chattering nineteen to the dozen.

Mary heaved a sigh of relief and made her way back to her temporary home.

'God protect Hubert,' muttered Mary desperately, 'and all those poor boys.'

She staggered up the stairs to her bedroom, still wearing the silly, ruffled morning gown and collapsed on the bed, too tired to undress and mercifully too tired to worry any more.

The next day, Mary found her servants inclined to be surly, particularly her lady's maid, a resident of Brussels, who was convinced that the French would beat the British and wondered why her mistress had not flown. The other servants were also locals and appeared to be dedicated Bonapartistes.

Mary regretted not having hired a lady's maid in England. She had always dressed herself, but on her arrival in Brussels she found that her husband had hired a local staff, and that included a pert lady's maid, Marie Juneaux. Mary kept to her rooms that day, resting and praying, no longer wishing to venture into the streets for news of the battle since, from what she heard through the open windows, the whole of Brussels was convinced that Napoleon had won.

The night of the seventeenth of June was miserable. Rain poured down in a steady deluge and Mary was more afraid for her husband than for herself.

She was roused from her prayers by the unwelcome visit of Lady Clarissa.

Lady Clarissa was not a coward and had not fled Brussels. On the contrary, the nearness of the battle and the scent of danger seemed to exhilarate her. Her cats' eyes flashed fire like emeralds and, in defiance of the atmosphere of fear and defeat, she was bedecked with jewels and wearing her best silk gown.

'I do not know how the men will survive this night,' said Mary miserably. Although she both despised and was jealous of her beautiful guest, she found she could not keep her fears to herself.

'Pooh!' laughed Clarissa. 'It will take more than a little rain to vanquish our brave Hubert.'

Mary stiffened at the use of her husband's Christian name, a fact which Clarissa gleefully noticed.

'Your fiancé,' asked Mary stiffly. 'Is he on the battlefield?'

'Perry? Good God, no. He is too concerned for the safety of his skin. Also he is a Whig, you know, and thinks it might not be too bad if Boney won.'

'For shame!' cried Mary, forgetting her natural timidity in a burst of outrage.

'Claws in, my dear,' cooed Clarissa. 'I said these were Perry's views, not mine. I do confess I have a soft spot in my heart for a soldier. Dear Hubert, so strong, so brave.'

'You knew my husband before our marriage, I believe,' said Mary, desperately wishing this woman would go away, and at the same time, desperately wishing to hear the worst.

'Oh, yes, *very well*,' smiled Clarissa languorously. 'One never thought Hubert would get married, you know. But ah me! The things men do for money.'

Mary rose to her feet and stood looking down at Clarissa, her large eyes sparkling with anger. 'You are offensive,' she said coldly. 'I have worries enough without your malice.

Please leave.'

'Oh, 'tis a jealous little wife,' said Clarissa rising languidly to her feet and patting Mary on the cheek. 'But it is the truth after all.'

'My husband loves me—and only me,' lied Mary, her anger giving her voice a ring of conviction. 'I am annoyed and irritated by your impertinence, that is all.'

Clarissa surveyed her for a few seconds, her green eyes narrowed into slits. Why, when the little thing was animated, she was quite beautiful. 'I shall lose the game,' thought Clarissa, 'and make an enemy of her. Hubert will take her part simply because she *is* his wife. He always was a bit of a stuffed shirt after all.'

She accordingly threw her arms round Mary and cried, 'Ah, you must forgive me. I was in love with Hubert once, Lady Mary, and I am still a little jealous. I have a wicked tongue and see how these rumors and dangers have upset me and make me say stupid things. Please forgive me.'

She stared appealingly at Mary, opening her eyes to their widest.

Mary was lonely and afraid. She was not yet aware that Clarissa was a superb actress. 'Please,' urged Clarissa softly. 'I am engaged to Perry after all, and I am not the kind of woman to become affianced to a man I do not love.'

Mary gave a little sigh. 'I forgive you,' she said quietly. 'There are too many enemies out there. I do not wish to have any at home.'

'Splendid!' cried Clarissa. 'Come now. I see a backgammon board over there. Why do we not have a game to pass the waiting hours and I shall tell you all the scandal of London.'

During the next few hours, Mary had to admit that Clarissa was extremely entertaining company. When Clarissa put her mind to it, she could charm both women and men. And Mary was still too young to realize that beautiful and charming people can often be quite nasty and cruel. She found herself laughing at Clarissa's stories. Clarissa did not mention Hubert again and Mary became convinced that Clarissa could not have been her husband's mistress. In her innocence, she believed that Clarissa's desire to please her and keep her company was ample proof of that.

*   *   *

Unaware that his wife and his former mistress were cosily engaged in a game of backgammon, Lord Hubert lay in the muddy battlefield and wrestled with his guilty conscience. He was old campaigner enough to have smeared his blankets with clay to waterproof them but, nonetheless, the unceasing pounding of the rain got on his nerves.

Tomorrow might be his last day. They had

36

held the French at Quatre Bras, but God alone knew how long he and his men could stand up to this ceaseless pounding. So many had already fallen. The Duke of Brunswick was dead as was most of Wellington's staff. Wellington himself had remained miraculously untouched, riding here and there in the very thick of the battle; his calm, deep voice urging the men on.

Hubert wished he had left a happy wife behind him. He had not meant to be so cruel to her, and now he wondered if he would now have a chance to return from the battle and make amends. If only the damnable rain would cease, then he would be able to pen a letter. He wondered what she thought of him behind that madonna-like mask of a face. Her eyes had registered a lost, hurt bewilderment as she looked down at him from the window as he rode away. But then, he thought cynically, any nicely-bred girl would look exactly the same after the sort of night she had endured. Perhaps she might not care if he never returned. That thought annoyed him. He did not love her but she was his wife after all and he did not want to think of her enjoying all the license of a young widow in the saloons of London.

The sky turned pale gray and the rain ceased as abruptly as it had begun. He sat up stiffly. A flaming red sun climbed up over the fields of rye, turning them as bloody a color as they were going to be before this hellish day was ended.

He looked across the fields to the small ridge above Waterloo and recognized the trim figure of the Duke of Wellington astride his horse Copenhagen. He was wearing his blue frock coat and a low cocked hat that bore the black cockade of England with the colors of Spain, Portugal and the Netherlands.

Hubert felt a lifting of his heart. The Duke had pulled them through so very many times when all the odds seemed against them. Surely he would do the same again today!

'I shall write to Mary this evening,' thought Hubert, rising stiffly to his feet. 'This evening will be time enough.'

*   *   *

The Brussels morning dawned. Knots of people stood around their doorways, dreading the arrival of the French. Rumors flew from mouth to mouth. The Prussians had been defeated, the English had been defeated, the English had won. And then the carts began to arrive.

They rolled into Brussels in a seemingly endless stream, carrying the dying and the wounded. Mary, who had been up all night, ran downstairs rushing from one wagonload to the other, searching for her husband, searching for anyone who might be able to give her news.

At last, she saw the white, drawn and bloodied face of Peter Bennet. 'Carry him into my house,' she cried to some soldiers, 'and anyone else you think I can help.'

She rushed back and roused her surly servants to action, crying for medicine and kettles of hot water, promising a footman a small fortune if only he could find a doctor.

'My husband?' she asked Peter Bennet. 'I know you are most dreadfully ill, but my husband . . .?'

I don't know,' said Peter faintly. 'Oh God, my head.'

He put a thin shaking hand up to the bloodstained and dirty bandage and moaned.

At that moment, the footman arrived triumphantly with the doctor in tow. Peter was pronounced not to be critical, although he had a high fever. The doctor turned his attention to the four other wounded men who lay in makeshift beds in Mary's sitting room. Mary frantically fought down her fears for her husband and listened carefully to the doctor's instructions. When he had gone, she busied herself attending to the wounded as the long hot day dragged on. And far away across the fields outside the city, the cannon of Waterloo began to sound, pounding and pounding through the heavy air. All day long the noise of cannons rolled, all day long Mary worked and prayed until she was dropping with exhaustion.

She had a brief visit from Mrs. Witherspoon, who soon lost interest when she found that Mary was not housing a title.

Mrs. Witherspoon was very sour. She had nursed a young man diligently all day, had given him her bed, and had paid the doctor, all in the belief that her patient was none other than the Duke of Hamden, only to find, when her patient had recovered enough to whisper his thanks, that she had wasted her time nursing a mere Mr. Hamden who was nothing more than a foot soldier. The glorious regimental jacket of the Hussars which had been draped round his shoulders had been put there by the sympathetic hands of his commanding officer.

By nightfall, the bells in all the steeples began to ring and the news was out. Napoleon was defeated. Waterloo had been held by the British and allies. Mary's servants promptly dropped their Bonapartiste sympathies and became tremendously pro-British, offering all kinds of help to the wounded, leaving Mary to fall into an exhausted sleep at last.

*　　　*　　　*

Lord Hubert Challenge rode wearily into Brussels on the following morning behind the ragged remains of his regimental band who were playing 'Rule Britannia' in double quick time. The Duke of Wellington had forbade the playing of the song for fear it might offend the allied armies, but Hubert hadn't the heart to check them. He was bone weary, exhausted. He felt they had suffered a crushing defeat rather than a victory. So many, oh so many, dead.

Beside him rode Major Godwin in the tattered remains of his evening dress. But the sun shone bravely and the fickle people of Brussels were all out to cheer the victors and suddenly Hubert realized he was alive. By some miracle he had emerged from that dreadful carnage, unscathed.

He stared wonderingly down at his bloodstained uniform and marvelled that it was not his own blood. 'Hey, be of cheer, man,' he called across to Major Godwin. 'Don't want Lucy to see you with a long face!'

Major Godwin brightened and his eyes began to search the crowds. 'She's probably billeted with your wife,' he said hopefully. 'I asked Lady Mary to look after her.'

Hubert felt an almost drunken sense of exhilaration, and his head reeled like the bells tumbling and clanging above in the city steeples. He reined in at his house and dismounted. As he turned round after tethering his horse, his first thought was to look up at the window to see if Mary was there. But suddenly a pair of white arms were wound round his neck and he looked, instead, down into the beautiful face of Clarissa. 'See

41

the conquering hero comes,' she murmured.

He threw back his head and laughed, laughed because he was alive and there were still pretty women in the world. He bent his head and kissed her.

Upstairs, Mary let the curtain fall and turned and stared blindly across the darkened room, darkened so that the bright sunlight would not hurt the eyes of the wounded.

Her love for Hubert, that first, fragile, tender and delicate adolescent love, withered and died. Mary was a very human girl. She thirsted for revenge. She crossed to the looking glass and stared at her reflection, at the pale face with the wide eyes and the demure wings of brown hair, then down at her fussy, frilly, outmoded gown. Her trousseau had been chosen by her mother.

As she heard her husband's heavy tread on the stairs, she muttered to herself, 'I shall become the most dashing young matron in London. Two can play at that game and a married woman does not have the same restrictions as a young girl. Damn him to hell!'

Peter Bennet sat quietly in a chair in the corner, studying the expressions on her face. He had been looking out from another window and had seen Hubert's arrival. He felt bitterly sorry for Mary, but good breeding stopped him from interfering in a marriage which was none of his business.

'*Mary!*'

Lord Hubert stood in the doorway, his arms outstretched.

'I am glad you are safe, my lord,' said Mary in a cold, formal voice. 'But be so good as to lower your voice. We have wounded here.'

Hubert looked around, aware of the other men in the room for the first time. Major Godwin walked in after him.

'Lucy?' asked the Major, staring at Mary, his eyes wide with hope.

Mary bit her lip, and Hubert saw her gray eyes were filled with pity for the large major. Then she walked forward and said softly, 'Lucy has left for England, Major Godwin. I insisted that she go. You did place her in my care, after all.'

The Major's face fell, but he tried to be fair. 'Thank you, my lady, I am sure that was the best thing to do. But it sort of casts a fellow down, you know, to dream of nothing on the road home but of seeing his wife again, and to find . . .'

'There were very frightening rumors,' interrupted Mary gently. 'At one point it seemed almost certain that we had been defeated. Practically everyone was trying to flee. It was best that she should go.'

'Yes, but *you* waited,' pointed out the Major miserably.

'Then you must blame me,' said Mary with a cheerfulness she did not feel. 'I am afraid I all but *forced* your wife into the carriage. Now, sit

43

down here by me and tell me about the battle and I shall send one of my servants to your lodgings to fetch you fresh linen.'

Hubert watched her as she listened intently to the Major as if he were the only man in the room. He found himself becoming very angry indeed. She should have been bustling about in a wifely manner, fetching *him* fresh clothes and seeing to his needs.

At last he could not bear it any longer and interrupted them with, 'If you will excuse my wife, Major Godwin, I would like some words with her in private.'

'Of course,' mumbled the Major guiltily. 'Forgot.'

Hubert led Mary into the bedroom and slammed the door. 'Well, madam,' he grated. 'Would you care to explain the coldness of my welcome?'

'What else could it be but cold?' said Mary lightly. 'There is no love in our marriage as you have often pointed out.'

'Your duty as a wife . . .'

'My duty, sirrah,' said Mary tartly, 'has been amply fulfilled. You have saved your family home through the marriage settlements. You have my money and that, my lord, is all you are going to get. I shall not interfere with your pleasures.'

'How dare you! You lay in my arms not so many nights ago.'

Mary winced. 'You do not love me,' she said

44

flatly.

Hubert shook his head wearily. He felt he should apologize but it was not in the nature of his class to apologize for anything at all—particularly to one's wife.

'I find this shrewish discussion fatiguing,' he said, beginning to strip off his clothes. 'We must be in Paris in twelve days.'

'You,' said Mary evenly, 'can go to Paris or go to hell for all I care. I shall be in London.'

He whipped round and struck her across the face. She looked at him coldly and then turned on her heel and slammed the door.

He started after her to beg forgiveness. But what was the use. She was a woman, after all. And women never understood anything anyway. He was sorry he had struck her. The room suddenly seemed to swirl in front of him. God, he was tired! Mary must understand he was suffering from nerves and battle fatigue. He would make things all right with her. Just as soon as he had an hour's sleep. That was all he needed.

*   *   *

The clocks of Brussels were chiming eight o'clock in the evening when he finally awoke.

Mary sat on the cabin roof of a public boat and watched with dull eyes as the placid fields and quaint villages slid past. Across the fields, the spires of Ghent rose in the evening air.

45

Behind lay Brussels, with its smells of blood and gangrene. She was going home.

She was going to change. First she would go to her parents' home and demand money—money to pay for the best dressmakers and hairdressers in the kingdom. 'If a Clarissa is what he admires,' she thought savagely, 'a Clarissa is what he will get.'

A little nagging voice in her brain tried to tell her she was being too hard on him, that she had not given him a chance, that he had been battle-weary and at the end of his tether, and that was why he had struck her. But the louder voice in her brain crying for revenge, crying over the ruin of wasted love, soon silenced the other.

Down below in the cabin she could hear the clink of glasses and the loud, jolly voices of her compatriots, celebrating their release from Brussels.

'He has won his battle,' she thought grimly. 'Now I must win mine. No man shall hurt me again. No man shall touch me again.'

CHAPTER THREE

The Tyres, Mary's parents, lived a prim well-ordered life in a prim well-ordered mansion. A trim line of pollarded elms marched all the way up to the well-scrubbed steps. The lawns were smooth and shaved like billiard tables, and the neat, well-ordered patchwork fields seemed to frown under the unruly shadows of the large fleecy clouds romping in an indecorous way across a pale blue summer sky.

Mrs. Tyre was as prim and upright as her home. She had gone into mourning some twenty years ago for a second cousin and had affected deep mourning ever since, enjoying the interest it caused, but always failing to discuss the reason for her mourning weeds, merely sighing mysteriously, into a black edged handkerchief, 'Poor Albert.' (Albert having been the name of the second cousin.) Her figure was spare and straight, with never an ounce of womanly flesh to relieve her stern silhouette. She had a neat, prim mouth and well guarded eyes which surveyed the world from behind a barrier of thin, white eyelashes. She wore black mittens, winter and summer, and her pale, lavender-scented skin was cold to the touch.

She kissed the air some two inches from her daughter's cheek and remarked in her high, drawling voice, 'Do not, pray, fatigue me with boring battle stories, Mary. It's Waterloo this and Waterloo that, and one will be glad when one can return to the more important business of the everyday world. Now, why are you come home and where is your husband?'

Mary walked with her mother through the familiar dark square entrance hall which smelled of beeswax and woodsmoke. Mrs. Tyre kept fires burning in all rooms of the house despite the warmth of the sunny day outside.

'My husband is stationed in Paris with his regiment,' said Mary, removing her bonnet. 'I am come to ask for money.'

'Money!' A startled look flashed across the arctic wastes of Mrs. Tyre's pale eyes. 'We were exceeding generous with the marriage settlements.'

'I know,' said Mary, turning to face her mother at the door of the Rose Saloon. 'But I am a lady of title now, mother, and it is essential that I dress according to my rank.'

'Come in,' said her mother holding open the door. 'We cannot discuss such matters *devant les domestiques.*'

The Rose Saloon remained the same. Perhaps it had been rosy sometime in the early eighteenth century when the house was built, but now it had plain white walls with the familiar prim landscapes of country roads running straight as rulers into the middle distance; or long lines of poplars running straight into the middle distance; or an avenue of funeral urns marching away into the middle distance. A straight, tall grandfather clock stood as rigidly as any soldier in the corner, its heavy tick-tock seeming to issue orders to the seconds—'Left-right! Left-right!'

Mrs. Tyre sat down on the very edge of an

upright chair and placed her mittened hands along its arms, placed her feet neatly together, and surveyed her daughter.

'Well, Mary, you may tell me now. What is all this fustian about dressing to suit your station in life. Did I not furnish you with a monstrous elegant trousseau?'

A thirst for revenge had made Mary dishonest. She knew she had only to appeal to her mother's snobbery and so she decided to lie.

'I had better explain,' said Mary calmly. 'I was at the Duchess of Richmond's ball in Brussels . . .'

'Indeed,' said Mrs. Tyre with a pale smile of satisfaction. 'The Duchess of Richmond. Very good.'

'*And,*' went on Mary, 'I overheard the Duchess saying to her husband that the new Lady Challenge would do very well but 'twas a pity her clothes were so provincial.'

'Indeed!' exclaimed Mrs. Tyre in quite a different tone of voice.

She sat for a long moment in complete silence while Mary patiently waited for her mother's snobbery to do its inevitable work.

'Very well,' said Mrs. Tyre. 'I appreciate your good sense, Mary. I am glad to see you have finally come to appreciate your position. Your clothes looked very well to me but . . . alas, I must admit I am not *au fait* with the current modes. How much?'

'Two thousand pounds,' said Mary grimly, 'just to start my wardrobe.'

Mary had deliberately asked for much more than she needed. She knew instinctively that her mother would be impressed by the outrageous figure.

Mrs. Tyre's white lashes flickered rapidly, but she was too proud to say she was astonished at the amount. She felt, instead, a dawning admiration for her daughter.

'I shall speak to your father, Mary,' she replied. 'Now, why do you not go to your room and change for dinner. We still keep country hours you know.'

Mary rose and went upstairs to her old familiar bedroom on the second floor. She sat down in the old ladder-backed chair by the open window, and felt her courage desert her.

She had written to her husband's servants at their town house, informing them of her imminent arrival. She had now all but got the money she required to cut a dash in polite society. But, how could she cut a dash when she suddenly felt very young, inexperienced and unsophisticated?

Mary conjured up a vision of her husband as a cold, autocratic boor. The more she concentrated on this image the more it solidified in her mind, until at the end of some half hour's meditation, she thoroughly hated her husband and was once again hell-bent on revenge.

Her lady's maid, Marie Juneaux, who had sulkily followed her mistress to this foreign land, answered Mary's summons and laid out a fussy, frilly dinner dress of pale pink sarcanet on the bed and proceeded to groom her mistress.

Mary entered the cool, square dining room with its square mahogany table and prim, regiment of hard, upright chairs an hour later to greet her father.

Her father was fat where his wife was thin, but he contracted his bulk under a formidable pair of Cumberland corsets and, in general, contrived to look as prim as his wife. His shaven head was covered by a plain brown wig and he wore an old-fashioned chintz coat, a striped waistcoat and knee breeches.

He had a soft white face which seemed to be pinned in place by two short narrow lines for the eyes, one short narrow vertical line for the nose and one long, thin horizontal line for the mouth. Mary had never really known her father, and often wondered if she ever would.

He did not ask her how she was after her journey, or waste any time at all on social chit-chat, but went straight to the point. 'Your mother says you need two thousand pounds to rig yourself out in style,' he remarked in that high drawling voice which was so like his wife's. 'And so you shall have it. Never let it be said that a Tyre was not of the first stare.'

'Thank you, father,' murmured Mary. 'I

51

shall indeed do the family name credit, when I am suitably at-Tyred.'

'Quite so. Now, come kiss me child, before we enjoy our dinner.'

Mary dutifully bent over him as he screwed up his face until all the lines quite disappeared into the flesh. He looked for all the world like a singularly tough baby suffering its mother's embrace.

He then bent his head and said Grace, and the Tyre family began to eat in their usual silence. For as long as Mary could remember, there had been no conversation at mealtimes.

A soft twilight settled down on the garden outside, and, one by one, the birds went to sleep. Mary remembered the clamor and noise of Brussels and the booming of the guns sounding from the battlefield. For the first time she enjoyed the peace and dull quiet of her home.

But she excused herself directly after dinner and went back to her bedroom only to lie awake for a long time into the night, nourishing her anger against her husband, so that she might draw courage from it. She could not hope to conquer the fashionable world, but at least if she tried very, very hard she could make enough of a ripple in it and bring a look of surprise to her husband's arrogant face.

*   *   *

With a draft on her parents' bank securely in her reticule, Mary set out for London a week later. She had never stayed in London in her life before, she and her husband having spent the first days of their marriage with the Tyres, and then at a succession of posting houses in England and the Low Countries on the road to Brussels.

The noise and dirt and bustle of the great city alarmed her and she shrank back against the squabs of the Tyre traveling carriage and wondered how on earth she was going to fare alone in this large city.

By the time the carriage rolled to a halt in front of the mansion in St. James's Square, she was feeling dirty and tired and defeated.

Her groom ran lightly up the steps to ring the bell, only finding, after repeated pulling on something like an organ stop, that it did not work. He applied himself to the knocker and at last the door swung open and the strangest butler Mary had ever seen stood on the threshold. He had a large squashed-looking face and little twinkling eyes like boot buttons. His livery consisted of a much darned, red military coat, worn over a yellowing white waistcoat and a yellow-white neckerchief.

His hair stood up like a scrubbing brush and was imperfectly powdered, making him look a bit like a porcupine that had strolled through a bucket of whitewash.

Behind him, a swarthy footman, who looked like a reformed assassin, was diligently swabbing the hall floor.

The butler made Mary a jerky little bow. Then he straightened up and saluted smartly. 'Name of Biggs, my lady,' he announced, staring straight ahead. 'Butler to my lord. Servants present and correct, my lady. 'TENSHUN!'

A strange assortment of servants filed into the hall and lined up for their new mistress's inspection. Instead of livery, all wore remnants of military uniforms. The cook was a large, bearded highlander with a white apron tied over his kilt. Mary was introduced to them all. When the introductions were over, she sent her maid upstairs to superintend her unpacking and asked Biggs to follow her into a saloon on the first floor.

'Biggs,' said Mary wonderingly, 'are there no female servants employed in this household?'

'No, my lady,' barked Biggs, springing to attention. 'All of us is soldiers what was invalided home after the Peninsula so Captain Challenge—he was a captain then, my lady—he says he can't pay us much but he can house us and feed us and give us these here jobs.'

Biggs suddenly ran his thick hands through his hair making it stand more on end than ever, producing a small cloud of flour dust. 'See here, my lady,' he said anxiously, looking full at Mary for the first time. 'We're a rough and ready lot, ma'am, and we've not been in the way of being servants except to His Majesty, King George, so to speak and God bless him, but we has kept the house as clean as a pin.'

Mary looked about her. The saloon was very large. The floor was scrubbed and bare. A few dingy, dark paintings ornamented the faded wallpaper, and a few ancient chairs stood about the room, looking as if they had dropped in a century ago for a visit and had not yet summoned up the social courage to leave. The room was dominated by a vast black marble fireplace depicting the rape of some unfortunate Greek maidens who screamed soundlessly into the long room.

'How can I become fashionable with such unfashionable servants as these?' thought Mary. But, sheltered as her life had been, she had heard many stories of soldiers starving in the gutters of London when their country no longer needed them. So instead, she cleared her throat nervously and said, 'Yes, I can see the house is very clean, Biggs, but sorely in need of carpets and curtains and furniture. Also, you must order livery *immediately* for yourself and the other servants. This day, I shall make good your wages. You will be paid as fits your station in this household.'

'Thank you, my lady,' said Biggs, and to Mary's embarrassment she thought she heard the sound of tears at the back of the butler's voice. 'We never thought for a minute you would let us stay, ma'am. I took a ball in the chest at Salamanca and it's still in there somewhere.'

He stiffly saluted. 'Just you give orders and we will follow them out, ma'am—my lady. Stand by you to the death, we will. Lay down our lives for you!'

Mary felt a lump in her own throat but she answered quietly. 'I shall indeed need your help, Biggs. I am determined to surprise your master by becoming the fashion. I shall need to set up my stables since he is still in Paris. I must also find a good dressmaker, which is really why I would have liked to see some female member of the staff. My own maid is still new to London.'

Biggs's face lit up with genuine joy at being able to help. 'James, the first footman, my lady, him what got it in the leg at Vittoria, is a-courting a housemaid at the Duchess of Badmont's. I'll send him there directly and he will find your ladyship all necessary directions. As to your stables, ma'am, you can't do better than to ask John, the groom who looked after the best horses in the cavalry and he got his in the arm, my lady, at Badajoz. I knows Gilberts is the best warehouse for furnishings, my lady, and I shall have a gent from that there establishment call any time you wish. We are sparse on provisions in the kitchens, my lady, so if you were desirous of a tasty dinner, it would be . . .'

'Send all bills to my mother and father,' said Mary firmly, 'and order all that is necessary for the kitchens.' She sent up a private prayer that her parents' snobbery would honor the bills. 'I am sure you will prove a good general, Biggs.'

Biggs saluted. 'Sergeant, my lady. Sergeant Biggs it is.'

Mary dismissed him with a nod of her head and Biggs clattered joyfully off down the stairs, his heavy boots doing a sort of clog hornpipe.

Mary rested her chin on her hand and prayed for courage. Perhaps she was lucky in these strange servants. A fashionable butler would not have been nearly so sympathetic.

'I shall become fashionable,' she vowed, 'even if I kill myself in the process.'

And during the next few weeks, she indeed thought at times she might die from exhaustion. The house was jam-packed from morning to night with a succession of dressmakers, milliners, haberdashers, decorators, carpenters and grocers.

Many cards were deposited on the hall table, but Mary did not yet feel ready to venture into society. The court hairdresser himself cropped her long hair into a short cap of saucy curls, and although Marie Juneaux, the lady's maid, assured her mistress it was all the crack, Mary felt very strange, getting a shock every time she caught her reflection in the looking glass.

At last the day arrived when she felt ready to receive visitors. She informed Biggs— resplendent in a new claret and silver livery— that she was 'at home'.

The house was not as large as many of the other London town houses, but it had a certain quiet charm. The ground floor boasted two public rooms, a study and a library, the first floor, four connecting saloons, each now decorated in a different color, the third floor held the bedrooms, including a new suite for his lordship and one for her ladyship, as well as the guest bedrooms, and the top floor, a chain of attics.

The saloon where Mary had first interviewed Biggs was now called the Green Saloon, its walls now panelled in green watered silk. The black marble fireplace was still there but did not seem so grim, now that the rest of the room was softened by rugs and vases of flowers and *objets d'art*. Brussels-lace curtains floated beside the open windows, for the weather remained sunny and warm.

Mary now sat in the Green Saloon. Her cropped hair had given her face an elfin look, and her gray eyes looked larger than ever. She was wearing a deceptively simple white muslin dress, tied under the bosom with long gold ribbons. The delicate white of her gown gave Mary a charming look of vulnerable virginity. She longed for a friend or companion to support her in her debut. In fact, she longed for any company but that of her husband.

All at once, she heard Biggs's heavy tread of the stairs. He had changed his thick-soled boots for a pair of equally thick-soled shoes and was so obviously proud of his new feathers that Mary had not had the heart to tell him that a good servant should be seen and never heard.

He swung open the double doors and announced, 'Mr. and Mrs. Witherspoon and the Honorable Cyril Trimmer,' and with a click of his heels, and a stiff salute, he clattered off, leaving Mary to rise and greet her guests with a sinking heart.

'La! Don't we look grand!' cried Mrs. Witherspoon, seizing Mary in a hot embrace. 'We called and called and you wasn't at home but Mr. Witherspoon says to me, he says, "Lady Challenge won't forget a promise not after the way we took care of Mrs. Godwin," so here we are.'

The Witherspoons were exactly as Mary remembered them in Brussels. Mrs. Witherspoon's bosom and turban were the same. Both she and her husband carried the same ingratiating leer. Their companion, the Honorable Cyril Trimmer, came forward to be introduced.

To Mary's inexperienced eyes, he looked a very grand young man indeed. His cravat was like a foot high snow drift, and his coat of Bath superfine had the highest, most buckram-wadded shoulders she had ever seen and was nipped in at the waist and very full about the skirt.

His waistcoat was embroidered with a whole covey of scarlet and gold pheasants and his very thin, very long legs were encased in lavender pantaloons ornamented down the sides with a multitude of vertical black silk stripes. His pale blue eyes held a calm contented look of absolute stupidity, and his sparse light brown hair was pomaded and curled and waved into an elaborate style. He had an eyeglass wedged in one eye so tightly that Mary could not help wondering if he ever managed to get it out. Mr. Trimmer had compressed his mouth into a tiny fashionable 'O,' from which emerged a thin, ultra-refined fluting voice. He looked as if his governess had made him practice saying his prunes and prisms for years.

Mary was very impressed.

He made her a very low bow, pointing his left foot with all the elegance of a ballet master. 'Charmed, Lady Challenge. Utterly charmed,' he said.

He sat down beside Mary on one of the new backless sofas, arranging his coat skirts very carefully. 'And now, Lady Challenge,' he began, 'you must tell me how you go on. Look here, interested in fine women, don't you see. Ecod!'

Having made this speech, he relapsed into silence.

Biggs and two of the footmen entered, bearing trays of cakes and wine. Mrs. Witherspoon stared at the servants avidly as they thrust the trays in front of her with military precision. Then having seen that Mrs. Witherspoon and the other guests were served, they wheeled about, formed a line and filed out before Biggs, who stood grimly at the door as if taking a march past.

'Shoulders back! Heads up, men!' rapped Biggs, swinging into line behind the last of them.

'Well, I never did!' crowed Mrs. Witherspoon in amazement. 'What odd servants!'

'They are all ex-soldiers,' said Mary gently.

'Oooh! You must be careful, my dear,' cried Mrs. Witherspoon. 'These men come from the gutter. Very useful when there's a war on but after all . . .'

'After all, I do not know what I would have done without them,' said Mary firmly. 'I have never known such a loyal hard-working bunch of men before.'

Mary listened in surprise to the sound of her own voice. She had never taken a social stand on anything before. But she had just done it and, although Mrs. Witherspoon's habitual leer seemed a trifle fixed, the heavens hadn't fallen in. Suddenly Mary found that her new gown did not feel in the least strange, and she caught a glimpse of herself in a looking glass on the opposite wall and saw to her surprise that she actually looked quite fashionable. She realized that she had not answered Mr. Trimmer's question.

'I have not been anywhere,' she confessed. 'I have been putting things in order here and I had to arrange a new wardrobe since my old one was sadly unfashionable.'

'I think you are very fashionable,' said Mr. Trimmer. 'I am accounted an expert in such matters, Lady Challenge. Permit me to be your escort and guide in society.'

Mary blinked and then recovered her composure. She had been about to point out that she was married but surely, this very fashionable young man was just the sort of person she needed to show her husband that she could attract a splendid member of the *beau monde*.

She smiled and thanked him, and then caught a little triumphant look that flashed between Mr. and Mrs. Witherspoon and wondered why.

She did not know that the acute social climbing Witherspoons had quickly divined Mr. Trimmer's problem. He wished a young lady to squire around to save himself from the unfashionable stigma of effeminacy. Unfortunately, he had very little fortune, although he was related to a duke, and fashionable young ladies were apt to dislike his posturing. The Witherspoons had promised to find him just the young lady to suit his needs and of course, should his noble relative, the duke, ever consider inviting them to a little soirée or something of that nature, they would be grateful to accept an invitation. They decided to strike while the iron was hot.

'We are making up a little party tonight,' said Mr. Witherspoon. 'A little evening at the opera and supper afterwards. Mrs. Godwin is our guest. Her husband is still in foreign parts.'

'Yes, indeed,' burst in his wife. 'Poor little Mrs. Godwin. She does hang around us so. Of course, we did say to her not to feel under any obligation to us, although we did arrange for her to leave Brussels but, I declare, she loves us for ourselves alone.'

'Ecod! I say, who wouldn't?' put in Mr. Trimmer gallantly.

Mary thought quickly. She did not want to go with the Witherspoons nor did she want to see Lucy again. But she did so long for a little gaiety. The monster she had created out of her husband lurked always in the back of her mind. Why should she pine alone, while he frolicked with the *mademoiselles* in Paris and did not even find time to write?

She accordingly said she would be delighted. Mr. Trimmer indicated to the less fashionable Witherspoons that ten minutes had passed since they had arrived and that to

63

stay longer would, of course, be monstrous vulgar. He took his leave with many elaborate bows and great wavings of a scented handkerchief.

After they had all left, Mary ran lightly to her bedchamber to begin preparations for her social debut. She finally decided on a pale green lingerie gown cut fashionably low on the bosom, with an over-tunic of tobacco brown velvet trimmed with gold bugle beads. The hairdresser was summoned to brush her short curls into the style known as *à la Titus*. She debated whether to carry a lace muff, and decided against it, substituting a handsome painted fan with mother of pearl sticks. The hairdresser finished his art by placing a little coronet of gold silk roses on top of her shining curls. With great daring, she applied a little rouge to each of her pale cheeks.

When she descended the stairs that evening to where the Witherspoons and Mr. Trimmer were waiting, her heart misgave her. Her ensemble, which had seemed so elegant in the privacy of her bedchamber, now seemed shabby in front of the magnificence of her escort.

Mr. Trimmer was wearing a blue silk evening coat which was padded on the chest as well as the shoulders, and his waist appeared smaller than Mary's own. His face was highly painted, and his hair gleamed with Rowlandson's maccasar oil. His silk waistcoat was embroidered with brilliants, his knee breeches were skin tight and his white silk stockings had large clocks on the sides, and his legs appeared to have grown muscular calves, which indeed they had, his valet having arranged a false, wooden calf in each stocking.

His gaze, however, was more vacant than ever, and Mary finally realized that Mr. Trimmer was a trifle disguised, having resorted to the brandy bottle before leaving his apartments and therefore would not have noticed had she descended the stairs in sackcloth.

'Tol rol, Lady Challenge,' said that young gentleman, waggling his fingers at her by way of greeting. 'Tol rol.'

Mrs. Witherspoon again crushed Mary to her bosom while her husband leered fondly on. 'And if she isn't my own sweet love,' cooed Mrs. Witherspoon. 'I declare you are like a sister to me, so I shall call you Mary and you shall call me Marie. Little Mrs. Godwin is going to join us in our box. Now hant you got any jewels, dear?'

'I did not consider jewelry necessary,' said Mary, feeling that Mrs. Witherspoon's personal remarks were the outside of enough. 'I am sure you have enough for both of us.'

This indeed was true, Mrs. Witherspoon's massive bosom being laid out with gems like a jeweler's tray.

Mary felt suddenly depressed. Mr. Trimmer

was surely very fine but the vulgar, pushing Witherspoons were a decided disadvantage.

Mr. Trimmer however seemed much struck with Mary, volunteering that he thought her 'a deuced fine girl.'

And Mary, who was unused to receiving praise, blossomed under his flowery compliments and soon began to look forward to the evening after all. When she sailed out of the house on Mr. Trimmer's arm, her only regret was that her horrible husband could not see her at that very moment.

The short carriage ride through the cobbled streets was exciting, flambeaux blazing outside the mansions, carriage lights winking like fireflies, carriage wheels rumbling like thunder as polite society came awake for the evening.

The Haymarket Theater was ablaze with candles from top to bottom, and myriads of jewels flashed on bosoms and cravats behind the red curtains of the boxes.

Lucy Godwin was already waiting for them, escorted by a very aloof young man who volunteered the information that he was Giles Bartley. Bartley stared at the magnificent Mr. Trimmer through his quizzing glass, remarking loudly and rudely, 'By God!' He paid them no further attention, flirting desperately with Lucy instead.

Lucy at last turned her attention to Mary. 'Isn't it fun with our husbands away?' she whispered. 'This is our last evening of freedom, though.'

'What?' cried Mary.

'Shhh!' admonished several voices from the neighboring boxes for the opera had begun.

Mary sat in an agony of worry as Catalini's shrill voice soared from the stage to drown out the chorus and the orchestra. Was he back already? Was that what Lucy had meant? She tried to concentrate her attention on the stage, but the colors swam and blurred before her worried eyes.

*   *   *

Lord Hubert Challenge strode into the hall of his town house and blinked in surprise. The tiled floor gleamed like a looking glass, the walls were painted Nile green, flowers glowed from vases on occasional tables, and a new turkey-red carpet climbed the staircase to the upper floors.

He then focused his gaze on the splendor of his butler, Biggs, who stood preening himself in his new livery.

'Am I in the right house?' asked Lord Hubert wonderingly.

'Indeed that you are,' beamed Biggs. 'Missus—I mean, my lady—has put everything in order, including me.'

Biggs turned slowly so that his master could admire the effect.

'Very fine,' commented Lord Hubert dryly.

'Where is my lady?'

'Gone to the opera,' said Biggs, running his stubby fingers through his powdered hair and sending a cloud of flour-dandruff onto the claret-colored shoulders of his livery.

'Not alone, I trust.'

Biggs shuffled in his heavy shoes. 'Well, no, my lord. There was a kind of tailor's dummy called Mr. Trimmer . . .'

'Good God!'

'Zackly. And a couple of mushrooms by the name of Witherspoon.'

'I think I had better change and join my wife, if I can tear her away from that man-milliner,' said Lord Hubert grimly.

He mounted the stairs two at a time and was bathed and barbered by his valet while he stared around at the splendor of his new apartment. His favorite hunting pictures had been cleaned and rehung on tasteful pastel walls. His ancient four-poster bed had been hung with new curtains, and when he sat gingerly down on the edge of it, he discovered it boasted a new feather mattress.

He was pleased with the transformation, but at the same time he felt Mary might at least have waited for his return. He had not thought of her much when he was in Paris. She was a woman, after all, and women were subject to all sorts of fits and tantrums. He had only behaved like a husband, and she had reacted like a typical wife. He had nothing to reproach himself with.

At last, resplendent in dark blue evening coat, exquisite cravat and knee breeches, he set out for the opera to find his wife.

As he was entering the theater, he met a doleful-looking Major Godwin who told him that he too, was in search of his wife.

'We're a bit late,' said Hubert cheerfully. 'We'll take my box and then catch them when the performance is over.'

When they were ensconced in his box, he pulled aside the red curtains and, raising his quizzing glass, stared across the brightly lit theater. He could not see his wife at all.

'There's Lucy!' suddenly whispered the Major. Lord Hubert followed his pointing finger and gave a start of surprise. For seated next to Lucy was a vastly attractive young lady who could not possibly be the pale, colorless girl he had married. But it must be! There were the Witherspoons and there, by all heaven, was that court card, Trimmer.

At the same time, Mary looked across the theater and saw him. Her eyes immediately darted away and he realized in some bewilderment, that Mary did not want him to know she had recognized him. Then she turned and laughed over her shoulder to Mr. Trimmer—and there was no doubt about it. Mary was flirting! And she wanted him to know it!

He leaned lazily back in his chair, beginning

to feel amused. What a naive girl she was, despite her new appearance! Did she honestly think he could be made jealous by a fool like Trimmer? Obviously she did.

Then he noticed Lady Clarissa, with a party in a box near his own. He decided to go and flirt with Clarissa and see how his little wife liked that. He still felt terribly amused by the whole situation. The fact that his flirting with Clarissa would hurt his wife never entered his head. Mary was a woman, after all, and women naturally did not suffer from the same deep and intense feelings as men.

Major Godwin was already rising to join his wife. 'Don't know what Lucy thinks she's doing with that feller but I'm going to throw him out that box right now.'

'You would fare better if you threw your wife out,' retorted Lord Hubert lazily, but Major Godwin had already gone.

Lord Hubert made his way to Clarissa's box where he received a very warm welcome indeed. Viscount Perry was not in evidence, and Clarissa quickly vouchsafed the information that her fiancé was abroad 'on business'.

Across the theater, Mary tried not to stare. She felt shocked and miserable. She had built up a picture in her mind of her husband as a beetle-browed, sweaty, boorish soldier. She had forgotten he was so handsome, with those black wings of hair falling over his high-nosed, tanned face. She had forgotten he could look so elegant. Suddenly, Mr. Trimmer appeared silly, fussy, stupid and overdressed. When she had flirted with him, she had caught the amused and cynical look her husband had thrown in her direction and had blushed to the soles of her feet. She had hoped to make him jealous by becoming a fashionable young lady. How on earth could he find her fashionable, accompanied as she was by this fop, by two of London's most vulgar Cits and that silly, fickle beauty Lucy Godwin, who seemed determined to torture her patient husband.

Mary sat miserably deaf to the music, learning one of her first hard lessons—that you cannot choose your friends for any reason other than friendship. Choose them for reflected glory, choose them to help you cut a dash, and in the long run you are left looking very silly—and friendless.

She saw Hubert's handsome head bent over Clarissa's beautiful one, and all her misery fled in a burst of rage and her courage came back. How dare he! How dare he, on his first night home, flirt with that . . . that *doxy*. How could she be so naive as to have ever believed there was one ounce of good in the beautiful Clarissa? Mary clenched her fan so violently that the sticks snapped.

There was further humiliation in store for her. Her handsome husband was, admittedly, waiting for her in the press in the theater foyer after the show.

Admittedly, he was alone.

But he treated her as if she were some tiresome little cousin up from the country. He bent his head and kissed her hand lightly, wished her the pleasure of her company of friends in a light mocking voice which bordered on insult, and said he was going to Watier's for a rubber of piquet and would, no doubt, see her later.

There was worse to come. After her husband had melted off into the crowd, Mary heard a loud, carrying female voice declaring with awful clarity, 'Did you see the new Lady Challenge? Pretty little thing, ain't she, but no *ton*. And such company! Even Brummell couldn't bring her into fashion now.'

That voice resounded in her ears even as she sat at her dressing table later that evening, after dismissing her maid. She had taken off her cambric wrapper and was sitting gloomily in a near transparent Indian muslin nightgown. She might have felt less miserable had she known that the famous Beau Brummell, that arbiter of fashion and leader of the *beau monde*, had also heard the spiteful remark and had not liked it one bit.

There was a faint scratching at the door And she swung round. Her husband strolled into the room.

'God, I'm tired, Mary,' he yawned, beginning to tear off his cravat.

Mary turned back to the looking glass.

'Get out,' she said in an even voice.

The hand tugging at the cravat stopped. Hubert turned and looked at his wife. She certainly had become an amazingly pretty girl, he noticed, with her saucy brown curls peeping out from under a lacy nightcap, and tantalizing glimpses of her white body showing through the thin stuff of her nightgown.

'I know what it is,' he said with an indulgent laugh. 'You haven't forgiven me for that scene in Brussels. Well, I apologize. I kneel before you. I kiss your feet.' He suited the action to the words.

Mary jerked her feet under her chair and glared at him like an infuriated kitten. 'I don't like you, Hubert,' she explained in a maddening voice of weary patience. 'Do get up and stop making a cake of yourself.'

Hubert rose, hanging onto his fast mounting temper. He tried to kiss her cheek, but she ducked her head and his kiss landed on the top of her cap.

'Look, Mary,' said Hubert, standing back apace. 'I know you were trying to make me jealous this evening. But you must do far better than that idiot Trimmer.'

'I was NOT trying to make you jealous. 'Tis only your overweening conceit that makes you think so, sir.'

'By God,' he said. 'I've a good mind to teach you a lesson.'

'Don't you dare touch me,' cried Mary, leaping to her feet and backing to the other side of the room. She suddenly became aware that she was dressed only in the transparent nightgown, and a furious blush seemed to cover her whole body. 'You have my money,' she shouted, goaded beyond reason by rage and embarrassment. 'Must you rape me as well?'

'I wouldn't need to,' he said, becoming as cold as he had been hot a minute before. 'But I do not waste my talents on gauche, little schoolgirls who think they are cutting a dash by being escorted by the silliest fribble in London.'

'Just you wait!' howled Mary, jumping up and down with rage.

'I am too bored to school you tonight,' he said, walking over and casually flicking her under the chin. 'You need a lesson in how to behave like a wife.'

'You would beat me?'

'I would kiss you.'

Before she had time to retreat, he clipped her in his arms and forced his mouth down on hers. She struggled furiously to no avail, and then decided to stand cold and unresponsive in his arms. He relaxed the pressure of his lips and began instead to move them gently back and forth against her own until he felt her lips begin to tremble against his. She felt her bones melting and her senses reeling.

74

'Oh, Hubert,' she sighed against his mouth.

He abruptly released her and gave her a hearty slap across the buttocks. 'Good night, my sweet,' he remarked cheerfully, and striding out of the room, slammed the door behind him.

CHAPTER FOUR

The usual unpredictability of the English weather struck fashionable London. A greasy drizzle fell steadily, trickling down the windows of Mary's bedroom in sad little tears. The weather had turned chilly as well, and Mary's sheets already felt damp to her touch.

She felt tired and low and despondent. She had lain awake into the small hours, waiting in dread in case her husband should visit her bedroom; or rather part of her mind dreaded the visit and another small mischievous part hoped that he would.

When her maid, Marie Juneaux, arrived with the morning's post and the morning's chocolate, Mary settled back against her pillows to survey the sheaf of letters which were, as usual, mostly bills. Then a gilt-edged card caught her eye. Someone—Biggs probably—had written laboriously in pencil, 'delivered by hand'.

She picked it up and squinted at the

convoluted script, and then lit her bed candle and leaning over, scanned the lines and then read them again, as if she could not believe her eyes. The Duchess of Pellicombe requested the pleasure of Lady Mary Challenge at a ball that very evening!

Mary had not been very long in town—but long enough to know that the Duchess was one of London's highest sticklers. An invitation to her home was tantamount to a royal command. It was almost insulting that the card should have arrived at the last minute. But then, perhaps the formidable Duchess had only just learned of her existence.

She was not to know, until long afterwards, that she owed the invitation to the wiles of Beau Brummell. That fashionable leader had been determined to prove that he *could* make Lady Challenge the fashion, and had accordingly used his considerable influence on the Duchess.

A footman entered with a coal scuttle and proceeded to light a fire in the grate. The cheerful light from the flames soon danced around the walls and Mary began to feel very excited indeed. She had a new ball gown which had, so far, never been out of its wrappings. She lay back against the pillows and dreamed of entering the ballroom on her husband's arm, basking in the glory of his admiring stare.

Her husband!

She sat bolt upright in bed. He must go with

her. She could not go without an escort.

She rang the bell and when her maid arrived, began to dress feverishly. She ran lightly down the stairs to the dining room to find her husband had already finished his breakfast and was preparing to leave. She rushed into speech.

'My lord,'—she waved the gilt-edged card excitedly—'I have here an invitation to the Duchess of Pellicombe's. Do say you will go with me.'

Hubert stared down at the card and then flicked it with his finger. 'I see my name is not on the invitation,' he remarked lazily. 'In any case, I have other plans for this evening. You did say, did you not, that you would not interfere with my . . . er . . . pleasures?'

'But I must have an escort,' wailed Mary, staring at him with wide, shocked eyes. 'I do not know of any woman who could act as chaperone. I do not know any man who . . .' She broke off and bit her lip.

'Exactly,' said Lord Hubert. 'Your friend Trimmer. I am sure he will do very nicely.'

'But I don't want to go with him. I want to go with you. How can you be so stupid!' cried Mary, stamping her foot in exasperation.

'You must learn that you cannot insult me one minute and ask favors of me the next,' said Hubert in an indifferent voice. 'The fact remains that I am not going with you.'

He gave her a slight bow and strode from

the room, leaving Mary to burst into stormy tears.

Mary bitterly wondered what was happening to her.

She was behaving like a spoilt child. She had been disappointed before, many times, and each of those times she had borne her disappointment with stoic calm.

'What is happening to me?' she wailed out loud, clutching a sodden piece of cambric handkerchief.

'I'm sure I don't know, my lady,' came the voice of Biggs from the sideboard. Mary turned round. Through a mist of tears, she saw the broad back of her butler, his head bent over a dish of grilled kidneys which he was examining with intense concentration.

'Oh, I didn't know you were in the room, Biggs,' said Mary, trying to recover.

Had Biggs been a properly trained butler of many years standing, he would have bowed and left the room. But he was not. He was an old soldier with an ugly, pudgy face and a graceless, stocky body—and a heart as big as St. James's Square. So instead, he edged nearer to the table and said in a hushed voice, 'If there is anything I can do to help, my lady . . . anything at all.'

Mary ran distracted fingers through her mop of curls. 'I can't tell you, Biggs. It's something you can't help me with. I can't possibly tell you.' Mary's voice choked.

78

'There, there, my lady,' said Biggs. 'You tell old Biggsy and you'll feel better.'

And Mary did. Mary who had never discussed anything with a servant in her life since her mama had taught her that to do so would be vulgar in the extreme and, furthermore, would cause a revolution among the 'lower orders'.

Biggs listened carefully, his great head on one side and then an unholy twinkle lit up his small eyes.

'Well, now, my lady,' he said slowly. 'I might just have the answer to your problem but you'll probably not like it.'

'Oh, I will! I will!' cried Mary, grasping hold of the butler's hand.

'See now,' said Biggs awkwardly, 'it's like this. When I was in the army, we had a lot of them there theatricals and me and some of the lads used to dress up and act in the plays, seeing as how the Duke, God bless 'im, liked a bit of theatre around the camp.

'Now in one of them plays, I took the part of a Spanish lady of quality. I was the Marquise Elvira Dobones deLorca y Viedda y Crummers. One of the officers wrote the play. Very naughty it was an' all. I still have the costume belowstairs. Very grand costume it is, too, for it belonged originally to one of them great Spanish ladies. So, if I were to put it on and keep me trap shut, and sit with the chaperones, you could go to your ball. 'Course,

79

we musn't tell his lordship for though he's the finest man in the English army, he can be a bit of a tartar.'

'It would never do,' said Mary dismally, while her eyes began to fill with tears again. 'It . . .'

'What the hell is going on here?'

Lord Hubert stood glaring from the doorway. Mary became aware she was still clutching the butler's hand and blushed fiery red.

'My lady had something in her eye and I was endeavoring for to take it out,' said Biggs woodenly.

'Really?' commented his lordship cynically. Then his shrewd eyes noticed his wife's tear-stained face. He walked towards the table and stood over her.

'I gather you have been crying like Cinderella, because you cannot go to the ball. Very well then, my child. If it means so much to you, I shall take you.'

But a few minutes ago Mary would have thrown herself into his arms had he volunteered to escort her. But now, Biggs's sympathy had made her resent what she now considered to be a piece of autocratic condescension.

'I don't want to go now,' she remarked, wondering in amazement if her voice sounded as childish and sulky to her lord as it did to herself. Evidently it did.

'Sulk, then,' said Lord Hubert carelessly. And the next second he was gone.

'Now you've been and gone and done it,' said Biggs with gloomy relish. 'It would have been silly of me to go with you my lady. I don't know what came over me.'

'Oh, please Biggs . . . do try,' cried Lady Mary, while somewhere in the back of her brain, the old self-controlled, madonna-like Mary looked on in amazement at the vacillating child she had become.

*   *   *

Lord Hubert Challenge had dreamt of this sort of evening for a long time. Now he was beginning to wonder why he wasn't enjoying it one bit.

He was ensconced in his club with a few of his favorite military friends. The play was deep, the wine was good, and a huge log fire crackled in the club fireplace, dispersing the unseasonable chill of the evening. For the drizzle had changed to a downpour, slashing against the windows, driven by a wild gale. He was both comfortable and fashionably dressed in a double-breasted tailcoat with a deep M-shaped collar, short-waisted waistcoat and close fitting knee-breeches. He had run into the Duke of Pellicombe earlier in the day and the Duke had been almost alarmingly effusive in his apologies. He would deem it a tremendous honor if Challenge would but grace his wife's little ball. Hubert had said firmly that he had a previous commitment but had, nonetheless, accepted the card which the Duke had pressed upon him.

He shifted slightly in his chair and he could feel the stiff edges of the card in his pocket pressing against his hip. Well, he had offered to escort her, hadn't he? And she had refused, hadn't she? And furthermore, she was a silly chit and he didn't care a rap for her . . . did he? But she was his wife and dammit, he had to admit he had not liked to see her cry.

He abruptly stood up and walked to the window and stared out into the street where a lamplighter battled with the gale, nipping up and down the posts like a monkey, filling the lamps from his oil can. The cowls on the chimney tops spun round and round, sending streams of black smoke down into the rain-drenched street below.

All at once he remembered the rain-soaked fields of Waterloo. He turned and looked at his group of friends round the card table. How few of them had survived! All at once the screams of the wind were the screams of the wounded and dying. Damn it all! He was blue-devilled. He would go to the ball after all.

When he arrived at his house to deliver the news to his wife, it was to discover with some anger that she had left. Asked who was escorting her, his footman became shifty-looking and muttered that it was by some Spanish lady.

'Probably some mushroom friend that the Witherspoons picked up in Brussels,' he thought haughtily.

He changed quickly into his ball dress, allowed his thick black hair to be teased into the artistic disorder of a style called *coup de vent*, tucked his *chapeau bras* under his arm, and set out.

*   *   *

Some streets away, Lucy Godwin strode up and down the room waiting for her husband to get ready. 'I declare I do not know what is taking you this age,' she stormed. 'I had as well gone with young Haverstock. He dances so exquisitely. Do you remember . . .?'

'Young Haverstock died with a ball in his heart,' said Major Godwin as he struggled with the intricacies of his cravat.

Lucy bit her lip in vexation. 'Now you have upset me by talking of death.'

'I am sorry, my dear,' replied the Major quietly. 'It seems as if death is my trade. I shall never forget that battle, or the useless waste. So very many dead.'

'Ooooh!' cried Lucy, bursting into ready tears. 'Are we to have no fun? You make me feel guilty. You prose so.'

The Major turned slowly. Large tears were

83

rolling down Lucy's heart-shaped face.

'There now,' he said in a softer voice. 'You are spoiling your looks, my sweetheart. Come, I am an old bear to depress you so. I shall be the happiest man at the ball tonight if only you will smile on me.'

Lucy gave him a petulant, watery smile. And with that he had to be content, although his heart was very sore. He was still troubled by feverish nightmares of death and disaster. But he was a mean and selfish brute to expect this fairy-like creature to share his grim agonies. Wasn't he . . .?

*　　*　　*

Mary Challenge found that she was able to forget her husband for at least two whole minutes at a time. She was the *succès fou* of the evening. She had entered the ballroom very nervously escorted by Biggs, expecting any minute that someone would cry, 'Imposter!' But it had all gone as smoothly as a dream. Biggs, a splendid Marchese in purple velvet, lavishly trimmed with crystals from the dining room chandelier, and with his brushlike hair covered by an enormous turban, had sailed off sedately to sit with the chaperones. Mary was quickly taken in charge by none other than the famous Mr. Brummell himself. She was at first overawed, but he seemed to find everything she said so excrutiatingly funny that she began to relax after her first surprise, and when he at last asked her how she was enjoying her first season, she found the courage to reply calmly, 'Absolutely terrifying, Mr. Brummell,' which sent the famous Beau off into whoops.

Her success was assured. Everyone was anxious to find what it was about Lady Mary which had kept London's leader of fashion so amused.

Without his patronage, most might have found her a pretty enough girl with her large clear eyes and saucy fair curls tied up in a gold filet to match her gold-spangled gown. But because of the Beau's obvious interest, she was at once declared to be 'quite beautiful' and her dance card was quickly filled.

Mary was determined to enjoy her success, and the only thing she found lacking was that her infuriating husband was not present to see it. Even the arrival of Lady Clarissa, who was dressed in silver gauze, damped so that it molded her body, could not dim Mary's enjoyment.

She was, however, slightly disturbed to notice that minx Lucy Godwin flirting with all and sundry, while her large husband propped up one of the pillars and watched. It really was too bad of the girl, thought Mary, smiling sympathetically across at him.

The next dance was a waltz and as Mary had not yet received permission to dance it, she decided to stroll over and join her friend, the 'Marquise'. But before she could reach Biggs, she was accosted by Major Godwin.

'I say, Lady Challenge,' he began. 'I must speak to you. Just a little of your time.'

Mary nodded and took his arm and they walked to the adjoining saloon where refreshments were being served. The Major found them a table in a corner, away from the other guests. He sat down heavily and looked at Mary like a large, sad dog who has just received a whipping from its master.

'I don't know how to begin,' he blurted out at last.

'It's Lucy, isn't it?' asked Mary gently. 'She is very young, you know.'

'But dash it all, we're *married*,' groaned the Major. 'I try to tell her not to flirt with the other fellows and she glares at me and calls me an old stick-in-the-mud. I tell you Lady Challenge, it's no go. You're a fine girl but you cannot understand what it means to love someone desperately and not be loved in return.'

Mary's beautiful eyes filled with tears as she felt a sympathetic knot of pain in her stomach. 'Oh, yes I know,' she said sadly.

The Major fingered his sideburns and looked at her awkwardly. 'I say, I didn't know. You mean . . .?'

Mary nodded. The burden of her unrequited love for her husband was suddenly too much for her to bear alone. For in that second she realized bitterly that she loved him with all her heart.

'Perhaps,' she volunteered slowly, 'your situation is not as bad as mine. You see, Hubert married me for my money. He never pretended anything else. But Lucy must have loved you.'

'She did at first,' said the Major, covering Mary's hand with his own large one. 'Those were marvellous days. Then we came to London. After that she had no time for me. She . . . she said I had stolen her youth.'

Mary pressed his hand in return and forbore from remarking that Lucy Godwin had obviously read too many novels.

'La! How comfortable you look together. 'Tis said you are the latest fashion, Mary. So you are become like the rest of us. Setting up a flirt!'

Lady Clarissa stood looking down at their joined hands, her cat's eyes alight with lazy malice. Mary snatched her hand from the Major's, but not before her startled eyes had caught sight of the tall figure of her husband blocking the doorway.

'I doubt if I shall ever become so fashionable,' said Mary quietly. 'Major Godwin is a friend. You must not mistake friendship and loyalty for anything else, Lady Clarissa. Love is a different matter.'

'In what way,' drawled her husband,

strolling up to their table. He had only just caught Mary's last remarks.

Clarissa swung round so that the drying gauze of her dress floated out from her body, showing tantalizing glimpses of the white flesh beneath. 'Hubert darling,' she exclaimed, clinging to his arm. 'Your little wife was just expounding upon the virtues of love. She and Major Godwin make quite a fuss about it.'

'Indeed!' said Hubert casually. 'You must tell me all about it, Mary. We shall dance, I think.'

Mary rose to her feet, all poise gone. The sophisticated Clarissa and her tall, handsome husband seemed to belong together. Their eyes, as they surveyed her, held the same look of mocking mischief.

'I have no dances l-left,' stammered Mary. 'Only the waltzes and I have not yet received permission to dance those.'

'Then I shall find permission,' he said smoothly. 'Ah, I believe your next partner approaches.' He bowed and walked off with Clarissa on his arm, bowing and nodding to various acquaintances. He had not noticed her success! The evening fell in glittering ruins at her feet.

Her partner was young Lord Fitzwilliam, a dashing exquisite who usually only favored beauties of the first stare with his attentions. He danced smoothly and expertly, chatting amiably when the movement of the dance brought them together. He gradually grew a little piqued. The Season's newly risen star seemed unaware of his condescension, replying only in monosyllables to all his wittiest sallies. When the dance came to an end, and he was allowed that very English privilege of walking about the floor with her until the beginning of the next dance, he asked her flatly, 'I fear you are not enjoying the evening or my company either, Lady Challenge.'

Her gray eyes flew up to his face in startled wonder and dismay. 'I am so sorry,' said Mary contritely. 'I am tired and my feet hurt. I would normally be extremely flattered that you should single me out for such distinguished notice, my lord, but I fear I would rather be home in bed.'

Lord Fitzwilliam laughed appreciatively, long and loudly, drawing interested stares from all corners. 'By Jove,' he gasped at last. 'Brummell was right. You are an original. I declare, honesty shall be the latest fashion.'

And Mary, who knew she had said nothing witty, extraordinary, or funny was left to stare after him in a bewildered way as she was led off by her next partner. Lord Fitzwilliam hastened to tell a highly embellished story of Mary's honesty.

His group of exquisites were delighted. Honesty became the new thing. People began to complain of their corns, their disordered livers and their tight corsets. One young fashionable aspirant became so carried away by this new vogue that he told the bewildered Duchess of Pellicombe that her ball was 'curst flat' and got ordered home by the duke.

After the next dance, Mary glanced at her card and saw with relief that it was to be another waltz. She could rest and find out how the stalwart Biggs was faring with the dowagers. She was relieved to see that, since her husband's arrival, Biggs had opened an enormous ostrich fan in front of his face and kept it there.

'My dance I think,' came a well known voice. Her husband stood looking down at her. Beside him was the slightly flustered Duchess of Pellicombe who was still wondering what had gone wrong with her ball that people should keep complaining so. 'The Duchess has given us permission to waltz,' added Hubert gently. 'By the way, I trust you did not come unescorted.'

'Indeed no,' said the Duchess before Mary could reply. 'A most exceptionable lady. Very *grande dame.* The Marquise Elvira Dodones deLorca y Viedda y Crummers, no less.'

'The *what?*' Hubert's eyes raked the line of chaperones. 'You must present me, Mary. Where did you find this lady?'

'I m-met her in Brussels after you had g-gone,' lied Mary wildly. 'B-but I want to waltz Hubert. I shall introduce you afterwards.'

As they moved about the room, Mary tried to stand on tiptoe so that she could signal over Hubert's shoulder to warn Biggs. But Biggs had disappeared.

Then Mary suddenly saw Biggs. He was dancing with the elderly Colonel Fairfax and, as the ill-assorted couple drifted past, Mary heard Biggs say in a high falsetto voice, 'Oh, ain't you the one, Colonel. You must be a fair old rip!'

Mary closed her eyes and Hubert looked down at her curiously. 'Feeling faint?' he asked.

'Y-yes,' gasped Mary. 'Take me home, Hubert.'

'So I shall. Directly after you have introduced me to your Marquise.'

'She's . . . she's gone,' squeaked Mary.

The dance came to a stop.

'I say, Challenge,' roared Colonel Fairfax. 'Want you to meet this splendid lady. Fine woman, damme. The Marquise de something or other Crummers. Sorry, ma'am. Never could get my tongue round those names.'

'Call me Elvira,' simpered Biggs awfully.

Hubert made a low bow. 'You bear a startling resemblance to an old friend of mine, Marchese,' he said, staring into those boot-button eyes.

Biggs rapped his lordship painfully across the knuckles with the sticks of his large fan. 'I declare you're flirting with me, my lord,' he

91

leered.

Hubert's face went rigid with distaste. 'Your imagination does you credit, madam,' he said. 'Come Mary.'

But Mary had to be surrendered to her next partner and went off with many an anguished look towards Biggs. But Biggs's familiarity with Hubert had done its work. Lord Challenge had privately damned the Marquise as a pushing vulgarian—worse than Mrs. Witherspoon— and did not look at her again.

He propped his broad shoulders against a paneled wall and waited for the dance to end. Then he would take Mary home. She did indeed look white and strained.

He felt a gentle tug at his sleeve and found himself looking down into the lovely face of Clarissa. 'I must talk with you, Hubert,' she said urgently.

'Is it very important?' said Hubert, his eyes never leaving his wife's slim figure.

'Very,' she whispered. *'Please* Hubert. Where we can be private.'

'Oh very well,' he said reluctantly.

He led her out of the ballroom and across the hall and pushed open the door to the library.

'Now Clarissa . . .' he began impatiently, but she was in his arms, her own wrapped tightly round his neck and her thinly clad body pressed hard against the length of his own, awakening reluctant memories of old desires.

'What is all this?' he asked huskily.

'I want you,' she said in a low voice, her mouth inches from his own.

Hubert forgot about Mary, he forgot that Clarissa was engaged to another man. It seemed to him that since that terrible battle he had been living each minute of the day as it came along, glad only to be alive with all that hell and carnage behind him.

He bent his head and explored her mouth, his mind beginning to register with reluctant surprise that nothing was happening to his senses.

*   *   *

'Oh, please Major Godwin. Do find Hubert for me,' said Mary her voice breaking on a sob.

The ball had turned into a glittering nightmare for her. Her disjointed, murmured comments were treated as the height of wit. Mr. Brummell had made her the fashion, and London society would not allow her to be anything else.

'I shall fetch the Marquise,' said the Major.

Mary looked wildly towards the refreshment room. Biggs stood with Colonel Fairfax at his side. He was surrounded by a court of elderly admirers. He bent his great turbaned head and began recounting something in a low voice. His audience listened intently and then burst out into roars of salacious laughter. Mary shuddered. She remembered that her maid Marie Juneaux had told her indignantly that the butler, when he was in his cups, had the bad habit of regaling the servants' hall with a stream of warm anecdotes. And Biggs's pudgy gloved hand was tightly holding onto a large bumper of champagne.

'No, leave her,' said Mary. 'Just take me to Hubert.'

'He left with Lady Clarissa. That is he left the room,' said Major Godwin pulling feverishly at his sideburns.

'Oh,' said Mary in a small voice.

'Look here,' said the Major awkwardly. 'Hubert's the soul of honor. We'll look about. Bound to be somewhere around.'

They entered the hall in time to witness the arrival of Viscount Peregrine St. James, Clarissa's fiancé.

Lord Peregrine looked as unappealing as ever, despite the magnificence of his evening dress. His great hooked nose seemed almost to reach his blue chin.

'Where's Clarissa?' he demanded.

'We're just looking for her,' said Major Godwin so ingenuously that Mary felt a sudden stab of sympathy for Lucy. 'She's with Lord Hubert.'

'Is she, by God,' said Lord Peregrine unpleasantly.

'I think perhaps I shall not trouble Hubert . . .' began Mary weakly, but Lord Peregrine had turned his great head and summoned one of the footmen. 'In the library, eh?' he said after a low-voiced consultation with the servant. 'Follow me!'

They trailed awkwardly behind him as he threw open the library door.

Clarissa had been disappointed and furious at Hubert's coldness. She heard the steps outside, and thinking that with any luck it might be Mary, she threw herself again into Hubert's surprised arms and pressed her mouth hotly against his own.

The library door swung open.

'You harlot!' said Lord Peregrine thickly. 'I'll horsewhip you.'

'Can I depend on that?' asked Clarissa, her green eyes alive with amusement. 'Perry darling. How marvellous to see you.'

She ran forward lightly and tried to embrace him but he pushed her aside.

'I demand an explanation, Challenge!' his voice grated.

'I haven't got one,' said Hubert lazily, although he looked past Lord Peregrine to where Mary stood, clutching Major Godwin's arm. 'Do you demand satisfaction?'

Lord Peregrine flushed. He knew Lord Challenge to be one of the most notable shots in England and a fine swordsman. 'Don't talk fustian,' he blustered. 'I shall ask Clarissa.'

'Do that,' said Hubert with insolent contempt. 'And now if you will all forgive me, I will take my wife home.'

'No,' said Mary in a sudden burst of rage. 'Major Godwin shall take me home.'

The Major looked awkwardly at Hubert, but at that moment Lucy's tinkling laugh sounded from the ballroom. 'Oh, my dear sir, *what* husband?' she said.

'Yes, I'll take you home,' said Major Godwin.

'It's *my* wife, Freddie,' said Lord Hubert lazily.

'I shall not interfere between man and wife,' said the large Major stiffly.

There was a commotion behind them as the Marquise sailed into the hall with her entourage. 'Oh, there you is, my pet,' called Biggs cheerfully.

'Oh, Bi . . . I mean, Marquise. Take me home.'

'Home it is,' said the Marquise, the boot-button eyes darting from Hubert's mocking face, to the Major's stern one, to Mary's pleading eyes burning in her white face.

The Marquise gathered Mary in one plump arm. 'Come along precious,' she said in a gruff voice. 'Men, my love, are all a lot of rots!' And with that the Marquise bore her charge off into the night.

'Well, I'll be damned,' said Colonel Fairfax.

'Probably,' said Hubert, staring with hard eyes in the direction his wife had gone.

The Duchess of Pellicombe came sailing up.

'I trust you gallant gentlemen are enjoying my little *affaire*?' she called gaily. 'What think you, Lord Challenge?'

'I'm getting out of here,' said Hubert still staring at the door. 'This is a madhouse—a veritable madhouse!'

'Oh!' wailed the poor Duchess. 'Whatever have I done?'

But Lord Hubert had gone.

He walked through the pouring rain to cool his fast-rising temper. By the time he reached St. James's Square, his reason had taken over and he was feeling heartily sorry for Mary. She must consider him the worst sort of rake. She must be crying her eyes out. Poor thing. And she had looked so pretty and, dammit, he was proud of her. There might be more to this marriage business than he had imagined. He would take her in his arms. He would tell her about Clarissa. He would convince her that it was all over. Finished and dead. Feeling very noble he let himself in with his own door key and hastened up the steps to her room.

Empty.

It was four in the morning. Where could she be?

He ran down the stairs to the hallway again and was about to ring the bell, when he heard the sound of laughter from the servants quarters. He pushed open the green baize door and walked lightly down the shallow steps, his dancing pumps making no sound upon the stairs.

He pushed open the kitchen door.

His wife and Biggs were seated on either side of the kitchen table with two empty champagne bottles between them, laughing uproariously. Biggs's face had a scrubbed look and his hair was unpowdered, and his livery looked as if it had been thrown onto his stocky body from a long way off.

Both saw Hubert at the same time. Biggs leapt to his feet and stood swaying slightly. Mary giggled and hiccupped, and the tighter and sterner her husband's face became the more she giggled.

'You, madam, are drunk,' said Hubert furiously. 'What is the meaning of this?'

'Why not ask Clarissa?' giggled Mary.

'Biggs, you are dismissed,' said Lord Hubert, his eyes glittering with rage.

'Very good, my lord,' said Biggs woodenly.

'Shan't!' said Mary, leaping to her feet, staggering wildly and ending up falling against the butler. 'I *made* Biggsy drink with me. Made him, d'ye hear? I ordered him. Stuffed shirt. Stuffed stupid lecherous *owl.*'

'My apologies Biggs,' said Hubert coldly, not noticing in his rage that his butler could hardly stand. 'I understand you were obeying orders. I shall take her ladyship upstairs. Come, Mary.'

'Shan't. Stay with Biggsy. Only friend I've got. Biggsy.'

Hubert picked her up and threw her over his shoulder and marched off up the stairs, not releasing her until he reached her bedroom where he deposited her unceremoniously on her bed and stood looking down at her.

'Pig,' said his wife pleasantly. 'Lecherous piggy-wiggy-wig.'

'I shall talk to you in the morning, madam,' said Hubert. 'Get your clothes off. I do not want your maid to find you in this state.'

'What *will* the servants say,' exclaimed Mary with an awful titter. 'Pig,' she added flatly. 'Owl. Greater stuffed owl.'

He deftly removed her clothes until she was naked. She lay back against the lace pillows with her hands locked behind her head, and stared blandly up at him with drunken unconcern while the candlelight flickered over her body.

It was a slim body with skin like satin, and small high breasts. He felt his pulses begin to quicken. He knelt beside the bed and put a hand over her breast. She studied the hand, with its large sapphire ring, with clinical interest and then yawned. 'It should be through your nose,' she said clearly. 'That's where pigs wear them.'

His hand moved gently and slowly over her breast and he bent his mouth to hers, kissing her long and deeply and feeling waves of almost suffocating passion rise to his brain.

But the passion was all his own. When he at

last removed his mouth, it was to find his wife had fallen fast asleep. He lifted her gently up, and covered her with the blankets and then went slowly downstairs to the kitchen.

Biggs's hair looked wilder than ever, for he had guessed there was a confrontation to come and had gone and put his head under the pump.

'Well, Biggs,' said Hubert. 'How much did my lady drink?'

'Two bottles,' said Biggs in a low voice. 'Said she needed a laugh.' His little eyes peered shrewdly at his master. 'Didn't stop 'er my lord for she was a-crying when she came in.'

'Very good, Biggs,' said Hubert curtly. 'I understand in this case. But my lady is not to be found in such a situation again. Do I make myself clear?'

'Yes, my lord. Very good, my lord.'

Hubert stalked off up the stairs and Biggs sank wearily down and rested his head on the table. What a night!

CHAPTER FIVE

Mary crept slowly downstairs in the morning. She felt strung up and nervous. The storm had blown itself out and yellow watery sunlight blazed in at the windows, hurting her eyes and making her head ache. Her mouth was dry as dust and she longed for a cup of tea, since the thought of her usual morning drink of chocolate made her feel acutely ill.

Memories of the end of the evening came to her in bright flashes of color interspersed with long vistas of cloudy gray. She remembered arriving home tearful and distressed. She remembered begging Biggs to stay with her for a little and Biggs, who was cheerfully drunk, suggesting they should repair to the kitchens after he had changed, in case Lord Hubert should find them. After the first bottle of champagne, she remembered talking long and earnestly to Biggs about love and life. After the second, Biggs's stories had seemed excrutiatingly funny, and after that she could not remember a thing.

Tea! Fragrant Bohea in a thin cup drunk in a cool, silent room would put her to rights. She pushed open the door of the breakfast room.

Her husband was seated at the end of the table reading his newspaper. Biggs was not on duty. She ordered tea in a faint voice and he lowered his newspaper and looked at her. Mary had never realized how much noise a freshly ironed morning paper could make, and put her hand to her brow.

'That is a very becoming dress, my love,' commented her husband. 'Gray with touches of pink. It matches your eyes.'

'Very funny,' said Mary sourly. 'Must you crackle and rustle so, Hubert?'

'I am not crackling and rustling,' he said mildly. 'You are suffering from the effects of too much champagne.'

'Fustian,' said Mary, raising her cup and drinking thirstily. 'Pray return to your paper, sir. I am not in the mood for conversation.'

Last night she had been dying by inches because of love and jealousy. Now she simply wished he would go away. His strong aura of sexuality seemed to fill the room to suffocation. Nonetheless, some imp prompted her to add: 'Or perhaps you have some pressing social business . . . like entertaining Clarissa.'

'I am glad you reminded me,' he said putting down his paper. 'I am driving with Clarissa this afternoon.'

'You sit there as cool as . . . as cool as . . . as . . . as *anything* and tell me that you're going to drive out with that trollop!'

'Now listen to me, Mary,' said Hubert. 'I had a certain involvement with Clarissa before our marriage. It is finished, over and done. I wish to make it quite clear to Lady Clarissa that there must be no repetition of last night. I am doing it for your sake.'

'Not for our sake?' said Mary, clutching the edge of the table.

'For our sake, then.'

'I don't believe you.'

'If I returned your brand of trust, my dear, I would assume that you were hell-bent on setting up Freddie Godwin as a flirt.'

'Nonsense!'

'Exactly,' he said with infuriating calm. 'I suggest you go and lie down and . . .'

'Mr. and Mrs. Witherspoon,' uttered Biggs in lugubrious tones from the doorway.

'We are not at home,' snapped Hubert.

'Oh, yes, Biggs, I shall see them,' said Mary blushing under her husband's surprised stare. She opened her mouth to tell him of her promise to the Witherspoons in Brussels and then closed it again. He would surely consider her a fool.

So under his curious stare, she left to join the leering Witherspoons in the Green Saloon. They had Mr. Trimmer in tow and Mary suffered a most unpleasant ten minutes. The Witherspoons and Mr. Trimmer had learned of her social success and were anxious to stake their claim to her society. She firmly turned down their pressing invitation to go for a drive and subsequently endured Mr. Witherspoon's particular brand of emotional blackmail.

When the Witherspoons and Mr. Trimmer had taken their leave, she returned to the breakfast room to find that Hubert had gone. She felt strangely flat and sick. Why should she trust him?

She trailed wearily up to her bedroom and fell into a hot, sweating, nightmare-racked sleep from which she arose some two hours later feeling worn out and depressed.

Although all the shutters were closed, the house seemed stifling and hot, and angry bluebottles buzzed over the gallipots with a monotonous drone. She dressed with more care than usual in a light, sprigged muslin gown with deep flounces at the hem and little puffed sleeves.

On descending the stairs again, she learned with some surprise that Viscount Peregrine St. James was waiting to see her.

He was standing in the Green Saloon with his back to the empty fireplace. His hair was powdered and tied at the nape of his neck by a black silk ribbon. This outmoded fashion seemed to add to his brutish air. He surveyed Mary with hot angry eyes.

'If I had a little wife like you waiting for me I would not waste my time philandering with old loves,' he said.

Mary put a nervous hand to the little necklace of seed pearls round her neck.

'I do not understand you, my lord.'

'Your husband and Clarissa. She told me they were going for a little drive in the Park for old times' sake. Old times' sake be damned. I know where they are. They are lying in each others arms right at this minute in an inn bedroom. An inn off the Chiswick Road called The Green Man.'

Mary began to tremble. 'It can't be true,' she exclaimed.

'I shall take you with me and we shall

confront them,' he said heavily. 'My carriage is outside.'

'No!' said Mary wildly. 'I don't believe you.'

'You must,' he said with an almost pitying note in his voice. 'It is the only way. Unless you see for yourself, you will go on hoping . . . go on believing . . . like me.'

'I am loyal to my husband,' said Mary stiffly.

'But he is not loyal to you.' Viscount Peregrine's flat, reasonable voice convinced Mary more than blustering or rage would have done. Her heart seemed to die within her and she felt faint. Then the faintness was replaced by a burning feeling of rage and desire for revenge. At least all lies would be at an end.

'I will go with you,' she said flatly. 'Wait until I fetch my bonnet.'

Lucy Godwin slipped quietly away from the saloon doors and ran lightly down into the hall where she nearly collided with Biggs.

'Didn't you see my lady?' asked Biggs looking surprised.

'She is driving out with Lord Peregrine,' said Lucy hurriedly. 'I shall not trouble her this afternoon.'

'You should have let me announce you, ma'am,' said Biggs looking at her curiously.

Lucy's beautiful eyes slid away from his gaze. 'Yes, so I should,' she laughed. 'Do not trouble to tell her I called. I shall let myself out.'

Lucy unfurled her parasol and settled back

in her barouche, a malicious little smile of pleasure playing about her mouth. It served prim and proper Lady Mary right. She *deserved* an unfaithful husband! How dare she hold hands with Freddie! She, Lucy, would drive in the Park and enjoy the cool shade from the trees. Then she bit her lip. She had promised Freddie to go with him to see his mother. But there would be so many dashing gallants in the Park. Freddie must wait, as he had waited before. He would sulk, of course, but she could always charm him out of it. The barouche rolled forwards and turned the corner just as Mary and Lord Peregrine appeared on the doorstep.

*   *   *

Mary began to feel hot and anxious. She wished she had not come. Lord Peregrine was driving at a furious pace. He had chatted amiably enough to her, explaining that he had only just returned from France the evening before, as he skillfully negotiated the Kensington traffic. But once through Kensington turnpike, he had sprung his horses and had set a hell-for-leather pace down the Chiswick Road while Mary clung to the side of the carriage.

Flat, empty, hot fields flashed by on either side and then the carriage veered over as Lord Peregrine swung it off the road and down a network of country lanes.

'Please slacken your pace, sir,' cried Mary, hanging onto her pretty straw bonnet. 'You will overturn us!'

'Nearly there!' he shouted over the rushing wind.

To Mary's relief, the carriage slackened its nightmare pace, slowed and finally rolled to a halt outside a tavern.

'This is a common alehouse,' exclaimed Mary in surprise. 'You must be mistaken.'

'Unfortunately, I am not,' said Lord Peregrine bitingly. 'Clarissa likes this milieu. She says it adds edge to the excitement.'

Mary winced. She could almost hear Clarissa saying it in her laughing, mocking voice. She wished she had not come.

Everything was very quiet and still except for the dry wind rustling through the hedgerows and the creaking and rattling of the inn sign. The inn was low and thatched. There was no sign of any other carriage, but Mary assumed that the guilty lovers had hidden it round at the back, out of sight.

'Come!' said Lord Peregrine, jumping down and holding out his hand. Mary hesitated. In her burning jealousy and rage, Hubert, with Clarissa in his arms in some romantic inn, had seemed a reality when she left London. Now confronted with this silent hedge tavern miles from anywhere, she began to think the whole thing impossible.

'I was silly to come,' she began but Lord Peregrine held up his hand. 'Hush!' he said. 'I can hear that laugh of Clarissa's.'

Jealousy is a marvelous thing. Mary listened intently and could swear that she, too, had heard Clarissa's high mocking laugh.

Grasping her parasol firmly in her hand, she marched into the inn, followed closely by Lord Peregrine.

The tap was deserted except for a thick, heavy-set landlord who looked remarkably like Lord Peregrine.

'We are looking for a certain lord and lady . . .' began Lord Peregrine. Mary stared at the landlord hopefully. Now that she was actually inside the building, the whole business began to seem unreal. But to her dismay, the landlord jerked his thumb towards the back quarters of the inn. 'In there,' he said laconically.

Mary pushed open a low door and found herself in a short narrow corridor. Lord Peregrine was so close behind her that she could feel his hot breath on the back of her neck.

With her heart thudding against her ribs, she walked forward and pushed open the door of the room.

Empty!

Nothing but a low iron bedstead covered with a greasy quilt. She swung around.

Lord Peregrine had his back to her. He was

locking the door.

'Why?' said Mary through white lips. 'You tricked me. Why?'

'Revenge,' he snarled. 'I shall have from you what that husband of yours has been taking from my fiancée so freely.'

Mary began to scream. He studied her thoughtfully and then slapped her across the mouth.

'No one will hear you, I've paid the landlord enough,' he said. 'But I can't stand the row.' He began to tug at his cravat. 'You can take your clothes off or let me rip them off for you. When I'm finished with you, you'll have learned every trick I've picked up in about five hundred brothels between here and Rome.'

He moved toward her and she backed away, looking wildly around for a means of escape, but the only window was barred. Lord Peregrine put out a large, beefy hand and hooked it into the bodice of her gown. He pulled her into his arms and rammed his hot mouth down over her own.

With a demented strength she wrenched her mouth away and screamed 'Hubert!' her voice like a clarion call.

Peregrine pinned her savagely down with his great bulk. Her hat was crushed over one eye and he wrenched it off and threw it into the corner.

'Now,' he said between clenched teeth. 'Now.'

109

But it was like trying to rape an eel, he thought savagely, as Mary twisted and writhed. He held her down by the neck with one hand and drew back his fist to knock some sense into her when the lock of the door shattered in pieces as a pistol shot ripped the country silence.

Lord Hubert Challenge stood on the threshold, a smoking pistol in his hand and black murder in his eyes.

Lord Peregrine's beefy face which had been flushed a moment before, turned ashen.

'Out!' said Lord Hubert, jerking his head at Mary. 'Out and wait for me.'

On trembling legs, which were barely able to support her, Mary tottered past him. She clutched at his sleeve. 'He will kill you, Hubert,' she whispered.

'Get out!' said Hubert savagely, 'and don't talk fustian.'

Mary tottered through the taproom. There was no sign of the landlord. Out into the dazzling sunlight she swayed and collapsed onto the grass verge of the lane, covering her ears with her hands. Lord Peregrine was so strong, so brutish, he was probably massacring Hubert right now. She must run for help.

But still she sat there, wincing at each muffled thump and cry from the inn. Then there was a great cry and a long silence.

She heard a sound and looked up.

Lord Peregrine stood swaying in the

doorway of the inn. Blood was streaming down his face and one arm hung limply at an awkward angle at his side.

'Hubert!' she cried desperately. 'What have you done with Hubert?'

But he said not a word. He pulled himself 'round the low building, hanging onto the wattle with one hand until he reached his carriage. He crawled into it on his hands and knees and painfully took up the reins.

Mary leapt up to her feet and ran into the inn, visions of her husband's dead body flashing before her eyes.

Hubert walked into the taproom. His blue swallowtail coat molded his form without a crease, his cravat was spotless. He looked down into her anguished face with a smile in his eyes.

'Dear heart,' he said gently. 'What a mull we have made of our marriage.'

Mary fled into his arms, sobbing and crying. 'How did you find me? Why is Perry so bloody and you untouched? Oh, Hubert, I am so sorry. I should never have believed him!'

'Hush,' he said, holding her tightly and putting his lips to her curls. 'Lucy Godwin fortunately could not wait to tell me the news. Somehow she overheard Perry telling you lies. She seemed so disappointed to find me respectably driving in the Park, instead of philandering in Chiswick. Perry is all bully and bluster, but an arrant coward in a fight. Now have I answered all your questions?'

'Yes . . . no . . .' gabbled Mary quite overset. 'Do you love me?'

His brown eyes held the old mocking glint.

'Come home with me and I'll show you,' he teased.

Mary buried her aching head against his broad chest and sighed. Could he not have said, 'Yes'?

'I must rest my cattle,' he said holding her a little away from him. 'Let us see if this hedge tavern has a hair of the dog. You look as if you could do with one.'

'The landlord?'

'I . . . er . . . persuaded him to leave,' said his lordship, smoothing down the ruffles at his wrists. 'Ah, what have we here? French brandy no less. Probably smuggled.' He found two glasses and stared at them thoughtfully and then, producing a large handkerchief, wiped them carefully.

With equal deliberation, he poured two large measures, holding one out to Mary and saying in a peculiarly colorless voice, 'Now drink that down like a good girl. I shall ask you questions afterwards.'

Mary looked anxiously at him. 'But Perry tricked me, Hubert. You know that. What questions?'

'Drink,' he commanded, holding the glass to her lips.

She drank the strong measure in one gulp,

shuddered and blinked, and then smiled at him weakly.

He dusted a chair with his handkerchief and drew it forward for her. Sitting down opposite, he leaned back, his thumbs in his waistcoat, affording Mary an excellent view of his broken knuckles.

'You are hurt,' she exclaimed.

'It's nothing,' he shrugged. 'Tell me, why were you holding hands with Major Godwin last night?'

Mary flushed and looked down. She thought of the large Major and the pain in his eyes.

'It is not my secret,' she said at last, looking down into her empty glass. 'I cannot tell you.'

'I don't like you having secrets with another man.'

Her eyes flew up. 'You have secrets with Clarissa.'

'No longer,' he said. 'I explained all that, if you will remember.'

'Clarissa—she heard Lucy's story too?'

He nodded.

'Then she will no longer be engaged to Lord Peregrine.'

'Oh, I think she will,' remarked Lord Hubert in a bored voice. 'It titillated her no end. That sort of woman finds brutish indiscretions exciting.'

'And that is the sort of woman you have consorted with in the past? That explains . . .' Mary bit her lip. She had been going to explain that that explains his brand of violent love making on that night in Brussels, but lost her courage.

But he seemed to read her thoughts for he said gently, 'I have not yet made love to you, Mary. I do not count that episode as love.'

Mary looked at him in embarrassed anguish. How could he sit there so coolly discussing such things which were surely reserved for the privacy of the marital bedchamber? One did not discuss such things with the hot sun blazing outside.

'Poor Mary,' he murmured. 'So much to learn.'

He stood over her and raised her to her feet. She looked up into his eyes and then closed her own as his mouth came relentlessly down on hers.

The world swayed and spun. The floor seemed to disappear from beneath her feet and a heavy, drugged sweetness took possession of her body as his mouth moved against her own, parting her lips and exploring her mouth.

Still keeping his mouth against her own, he swept her up in his arms and carried her down the corridor toward the bedroom.

She pulled her mouth free. 'What are you doing?' she cried.

'Taking you to bed,' he smiled.

'To . . . It's the middle of the afternoon, sir!' cried Mary appalled. 'That bed, no doubt, is full of livestock and you want to . . . oooh!'

He dropped her abruptly to her feet. 'Not yet a woman,' he remarked coldly, his eyes like pieces of agate.

'Me, not yet a woman,' said Mary shrilly, hurt unreasonably. 'I may not be one of the strumpets you are used to bedding but I am a lady, sir, and I will not soil my dress on that filthy bed.'

'Oh, really,' he said savagely. 'Did you mean to keep it on? How quaint. Very well, madam. We shall return home and draw the shades and extinguish the candles and you may keep all your clothes on and, if it pleases you, I will go to bed in my boots and breeches, but have you I will.'

Mary was shocked. That anyone should dare to be so crude in the presence of a lady!

She folded her lips into a thin line and marched back down the corridor and through the inn. Then she saw with dismay that his horse, Vittoria, was tethered to a tree outside and there was no sign of a carriage.

'I could not bring the carriage to your rescue,' he said behind her. 'It would have taken too much time. With one horse I was able to cut across the fields. You must ride with me . . . on the horse I mean, my love, in case I have offended your delicate sensibilities with my boorish masculinity.'

She said nothing but allowed him to throw her up into the saddle. He mounted behind her and gathered the reins in one hand, holding her lightly with the other. She sat bolt upright, feeling faint at the sensations caused by that light touch.

The air was hot and humid and still, heavy with the scent of the hedgeroses, and the long shining grass still wet from last night's storm.

She wondered bitterly whether her husband could sense the churning emotions in her body, but he said not a word until Chiswick Mall was reached and he rode into the yard of a posting inn under the curious stares of the ostlers. 'We will bespeak a carriage here,' he said curtly. He swung her lightly to the ground and then turned and strode off into the inn, not once looking behind him to see if she were following.

Suddenly she remembered that quadrille on the night of the Duchess of Richmond's ball. Was she never to be free of Perry and Clarissa and the problems of Lucy and Freddie, not to mention the pushing Witherspoons?

*   *   *

'I am going to the opera tonight. So there!' screamed Lucy Godwin at her large husband. 'And if you need feminine company, I suggest you go and hold hands again with Mary Challenge!'

'I thought we might spend an evening together like the old days,' said Freddie

Godwin miserably.

Lucy stared angrily at him. He made her feel so guilty. If only he would shake her or beat her or do anything other than sit there like a great lummox.

But goaded on by the pain shown in his eyes, she went from bad to worse. 'Don't talk to me of the "old days",' she sneered. 'What a pair of little country bumpkins we were then.'

'Don't call me little, Lucy.'

'Little, little, *little*. Awful *little* man!'

The Major took a step toward her and raised his hand.

'That's right!' screamed Lucy, 'beat me like the brute you are.'

He dropped his arm and then said in a measured voice, 'Very well, Lucy. Have your fun. But show one serious *tendre* for any man and I will shoot him first and strangle you afterwards.'

'Mr. and Mrs. Witherspoon,' announced a servant.

Lucy stared at her husband uncertainly. Then, 'Pooh!' she said, shrugging a muslin shoulder, and went off impatiently to see the Witherspoons. Really, they were the outside of enough. She must tell the servants not to admit them.

The Witherspoons had their customary leer pinned on their large faces, but for once it did not reach up to their eyes. They had received snub after snub since their return from

Brussels. Money they had in plenty. But what they desired was social acceptance and they were prepared to get it any way they could.

After the tea tray had been brought in and social chit-chat exchanged, Mr. Witherspoon fixed Lucy with a steely gaze and said, 'I fear Lady Challenge has forgotten the great service we did her in getting you out of Brussels. Begging and crying and pleading you were. "What about your husband?" asks one lady. "Oh, I don't care," you says. "Freddie can take care of himself." Tut-tut. Society don't like that kind of behavior, Mrs. Godwin.'

Lucy sat very still. Society had indeed begun to circulate stories of those who had fled from Brussels, leaving their men to die on the battlefield. If the Witherspoons circulated such a story, she would be socially damned, and some of her best and brightest flirts were among the military.

'But you have not told anyone since we are friends,' she said at last with a lightness she did not feel.

'Not yet.' The two words fell, carefully measured, into the hot, still room.

'I am grateful to you for all you have done. Do you want money?' asked Lucy hopefully.

Mr. Witherspoon shook his head while his wife munched cake after cake, her eyes never leaving Lucy's face.

'It is not your gratitude we want,' said Mr. Witherspoon. 'We want Lady Challenge's gratitude. She is all the crack now, and it would be deemed a mark of distinction if we could be seen abroad with her. You must remind her of her social obligation.'

'Oh, very well,' said Lucy pettishly.

'See that you do,' said Mr. Witherspoon. 'Just see that you do.'

*   *   *

'You are looking particularly dowdy tonight, my love,' remarked Lord Hubert Challenge to his wife as they faced each other down the length of the dining table.

Mary looked down guiltily at her dress. It was of gray silk in an old-fashioned mode, with a high neck and long tight sleeves. She had suddenly been terrified of the night to come and had chosen the most repelling gown she could find.

'Do you wish me to change my clothes?' she asked.

'No,' remarked Lord Hubert lazily. 'Just take them off. What's the matter Biggs? Got a cold?'

'No, my lord. Must have burnt me hand on this 'ere chafing dish.'

'Then we are quite well able to serve ourselves. You may go to the kitchens and have it attended to and . . . er . . . Biggs.'

'Yes, my lord.'

'Don't come back, there's a good fellow.'

'Monstrous!' cried Mary after Biggs had gone. 'To make such remarks, and in front of a servant too!'

'You drive me to it, Mary,' he said, his eyes mocking her. 'Miss Prunes and Prisms. You are so easily shocked.'

Mary gulped at her wine and picking up the decanter, poured herself another glass.

Lord Hubert's black brows rose in surprise. 'Does your mother drink? Or your father?'

'Of course,' snapped Mary.

'I mean to excess.'

'No.'

'Splendid. I was beginning to fear you had inherited one of the Fatal Tendencies. Come and kiss me.'

Mary put down her glass. She was too frightened. Love should be a gentle and delicate minuet, not this constant assault upon the senses. She must have courage. She had been abducted, nearly raped. She had had insufficient sleep.

'Hubert,' she said desperately. 'You must excuse me.'

'You have a headache, of course.'

'Oh, yes,' cried Mary, delighted to find him so reasonable.

'Then you may retire,' he rejoined equably.

She looked at him doubtfully. He had changed into evening dress although they were dining at home and looked very splendid and remote.

'And where are you going, my lord?'

'Ah,' he teased. 'That is my secret. Come and kiss me, Mary!'

She walked slowly towards him. He lay back in his chair, his eyes glinting up at her from under their heavy lashes. She looked down at him and then stooped to plant a brief kiss on his cheek. He turned his head abruptly so that the kiss fell full on his mouth, and his lips seemed to cling and burn although he did not raise his hands to touch her. She stayed there for a long time, imprisoned by his kiss, feeling her head reel.

Finally he held her away from him with gentle hands.

'Go to bed, Mary,' he said quietly.

She hung her head and walked slowly away, feeling bitterly disappointed. Now that he was obviously not going to spend the night with her, she wanted his body pressed against her own more than anything in the world.

Juneaux chattered away as she unpinned her mistress's hair and prepared her for bed, but Mary only replied in monosyllables, her mind busy with the problem of her husband.

When Juneaux had gone, Mary climbed into bed and stared sightlessly at the canopy. The room was uncomfortably warm and sticky and smelled of sugar and vinegar from the gallipots. She threw back the blankets and restlessly stretched her legs. The flame of the candle beside the bed burned clear and straight without a flicker.

'It is not my fault,' she whispered to the uncaring shadows. 'It is too soon. I have known no courtship. I am frightened. But I need not be frightened for he will not come this night.'

Two restless hours later she heard his steps in the corridor outside and stiffened against the pillows. But he walked past the door of her room without a pause and seconds later she heard the door of his bedroom close.

She bit her lip, suddenly troubled. She could not expect a man of his caliber to remain celibate. He would soon find consolation elsewhere. She had a vivid picture of Clarissa, lying back in his arms, she groaned aloud. Was she, Mary, less of a woman than Clarissa. No! But a very inexperienced one, whispered a frightened voice in her brain.

Another hour passed while she tossed and turned fretfully. At last, she slowly climbed down from the bed. She would just look in at his bedroom. There was no harm in that. If he was awake, they could talk and perhaps she could explain her fears.

She gently pushed open the door to his bedroom and went in.

The bed curtains were drawn back and he was sprawled back against the pillows, fast asleep. The blankets were thrown onto the floor, where they lay in a tangled knot. He was stark naked, the faint yellow light from the oil lamp outside the window gleaming on the muscles of his back, which was turned to her.

She took a hurried step backwards and then stopped. He was asleep after all. He did not look so terrifying naked, nor so shocking as she had thought. His face probably looked softer and younger in repose, she thought.

She tiptoed forwards holding her bed candle high and bent over him. The long lashes lay on his cheek softening the harsh lean lines of his face. His long, mobile, sensuous mouth was curved in a half smile and the white-muscled column of his throat rose above the dark hair of his chest. As she bent over him, a drop of hot wax from the candle fell on his shoulder and his eyes flew open.

She retreated hurriedly. 'I had a nightmare,' she whispered. He reached out a strong white hand and pulled her roughly into bed, and then rolled over on top of her.

'Let me up,' she breathed. 'A nightmare, yes, that's what it was.'

He did not seem to hear her. His eyelids half closed, he simply began to kiss her, slowly and lingeringly until she groaned against his mouth. His lips moved downwards across her body, burning through the thin material of her nightgown, caressing and teasing, while his long strong fingers roved and probed. He made love to her slowly, sensuously and lingeringly, with a single-minded absorption, until she was digging her nails into his back

123

and crying out for she knew not what.

When he at last moved inside her, the bed began to creak alarmingly like a ship in a high storm, and she had a sudden, panicky feeling, 'What on earth will the servants think?' before her senses took over and she was never to know that even her delirious cry of fulfillment went unnoticed by everyone except Biggs, who opened the window and shied his army boots at a perfectly innocent cat who had not said a word.

When she awoke, dawn was pearling the sky and the watch was crying five o'clock. He was sprawled across her body and awoke the minute she moved and smiled down at her, his eyes very wide and tender. 'What are you thinking of, my sweet?' he whispered.

'I am worried about the servants,' said Mary anxiously. 'I should be so embarrassed to be found here when your man comes in with your chocolate in the morning.'

Did he look disappointed or was it a trick of the light?

'Then I shall escort you to your own room, my prude,' he said, climbing out of bed and shrugging into his dressing gown.

'You *do* understand,' pleaded Mary, feeling she had said entirely the wrong thing. She should have told him she loved him, which she did, but at that moment she could not bring herself to say so.

He opened the door of her bedroom and

ushered her in.

'Goodnight, my sweet,' he said, looking down at her. 'You kept your clothes on after all . . . or nearly on.'

She looked down at her crumpled nightdress and blushed. He put out a long finger and tilted her face up to his.

It seemed that seconds later she was in his arms, he was in her bed, and her nightgown lay crumpled in a ball in the corner of the room where it had been thrown by an impatient hand.

'Bleeding cats,' said Biggs, throwing up the sash and poking his rifle through the bars.

Juneaux nearly dropped her mistress's tray of chocolate when she blithely marched into the room in the morning, stopping short in amazement at the sight of the tangled figures on the bed.

Pursing her lips in disapproval, she turned about and marched out. The English were so indecorous!

*   *   *

'Hubert, it is noon,' wailed Mary some time later. 'Oh, my goodness, Juneaux must have seen us.'

'Fascinating,' said her lord lazily. 'You blush all over. Noon is it? Then let us celebrate the dawning of the afternoon.'

'Oh, Hubert. No, we can't possibly . . .'

'*Darling!*'

'Oh, Hubert!'

Two hours later, Mary awoke feeling dizzy and light-headed.

'Hubert. I am so hungry.'

'A healthy sign. So am I. I shall eat your left ear.'

'Please don't, darling. This is impossible. You know quite well I did not mean that sort of hunger. My lord, I pray you listen to me. Only think of the servants. Only think of the . . . Oh, Hubert . . .'

They did not eat till dinner time. Served by an indulgent and cheerful Biggs, they made but poor work of their evening meal, drinking more then they should and staring into each other's eyes in sleepy fascination.

'We shall give a party,' said Mary, slightly tipsily. 'An Impromptu Party. We shall invite everyone. A great, big, beautiful party.'

'A party you shall have,' said Hubert sleepily. 'See that you are not overworked, Biggs!'

'No, my lord. It'll be like a campaign,' said Biggs cheerfully. 'I'll leave my lord and my lady to their wine.'

He went out and quietly closed the door.

Hubert flashed a wicked smile down the table at his wife. 'Come and kiss me, Mary.'

And she did. Long into the night while the candles burned down and the untouched food congealed on the table, and the tactful servants stayed belowstairs and Biggs laid wagers on his lordship's stamina.

CHAPTER SIX

Lucy Godwin paced nervously up and down Mary's drawing room, the sarcanet flounces of her gown swishing over the carpet.

'I declare Mary,' said Lucy coming to a halt. 'It is too vexing of you. Too monstrous thoughtless. Why did you not send the Witherspoons a card to your rout?'

'It is an informal, impromptu party, Lucy,' said Mary gently. 'They really only like grand affairs. I am obliged to them for their kind offices in Brussels but, in all faith, I cannot like them.'

'Like them?' sneered Lucy awfully. 'When did one ever have to like people to invite them? I tell you this, if you do not invite them, they will tell the world and his wife that I abandoned poor Freddie on the battlefield.'

'You imagine things. Surely they would not say so.'

'Oh, yes they would,' cried Lucy pettishly. 'I shall be socially ruined and it's all your fault. You p-promised Freddie you'd take care of me.'

'Only in his absence.'

Lucy burst into noisy tears. 'I think you're

horrid,' she sobbed.

'Very well then,' said Mary on a sigh. She was so happy she could not bear to see anyone else unhappy. 'I shall send them a card. But will they not be insulted? The party is this very evening after all.'

'Oh, no,' said Lucy cynically, her tears drying like magic, 'so long as they are invited.'

She slid a curious look at Mary's radiant face, out of the corner of her eyes. 'I declare I am surprised you should condone the presence of Lady Clarissa and her fiancé, Lord Peregrine.'

'You must be mistaken,' said Mary coldly. 'I sent no invitation.'

'Really,' said Lucy with a little titter. 'I would ask dear Lord Hubert about it. Goodbye, dear.'

She kissed the air somewhere in the region of Mary's cheek and floated out.

Mary went in search of her husband. He was sitting in his study brooding over a glass of madeira and nursing a blinding headache. That morning, while Mary lay asleep, recuperating after another energetic night, he found himself strangely restless. He had gone out riding and had come across an old friend he had thought dead on the battlefield of Waterloo. They had gone off to celebrate too much, and too wildly. He had returned to find his house in an uproar. Decorators were draping the saloons in swathes of silk.

Footmen were staggering around with potted plants. Strange housemaids hired for the occasion were flirting shrilly with his military servants and nowhere could he find peace except in his study. He slammed the shutters closed and decided to have a glass of wine, and then an hour's sleep, before preparing for the rigors of the evening.

He winced as his wife crashed through the door, two bright spots of color burning on her cheek.

'Did you or did you not invite Clarissa and Perry?' she stormed.

'Yes,' he said, 'and don't shout!'

'Is this some mad joke?' asked Mary, staring at him with hauteur. 'I would have thought that Lord Peregrine would have taken himself out of the country.'

'He had no need,' said Hubert curtly, suddenly disliking his wife excrutiatingly. 'He knew I did not want your name dragged into any scandal. I have no further quarrel with either of them. He called on me and explained in a very gentlemanly fashion that he had been driven insane with jealousy.'

'You should have horsewhipped him,' shouted Mary.

Hubert clutched his fevered forehead and groaned. 'Leave me alone, Mary. My hea . . .'

'No I will not leave you alone. You will send a footman round to Lady Clarissa immediately cancelling the invitation. Do you hear me?'

'I hear you, madam. The whole of St. James's can hear you, dammit.'

'I order you . . .'

She broke off as he sprang wrathfully to his feet. 'You *order* me. Who in hell do you think you are? Get out of here before I slap you to your senses.'

'You're a monster,' screamed Mary, jumping up and down. 'And . . . and . . . your nose is too big.'

There was a shocked silence.

He stalked to the mirror over the mantle and twisted his head from side to side.

'It is a splendid nose,' he pronounced at last.

'It's big! It's enormous! I hate it,' Mary screamed even louder, quite beside herself.

'It is a fine example of an aristocratic nose,' he said, glaring at her. 'I do not have a common feature in my face—unlike yours.'

'What is wrong with my face?'

'You've got a great long trap of a mouth. Vulgar, common, faugh!'

'Eh hiv nit,' piped Mary pursing her lips into as small a shape as she could manage.

'And talking of being common,' pursued Hubert. 'Why not ask your so dear friends the Witherspoons.'

'I will do that directly.' Mary burst into noisy tears and fled from the room, crashing the door so violently so that it rocked on its hinges.

She rushed to her writing desk and scrawled

a fulsome invitation to the Witherspoons and sent it off by hand. She then scrambled up the stairs to her bedroom where she lay on the bed and cried her eyes out. She thought she heard her husband's footsteps outside the door, so she cried even louder but all she heard in reply was the slamming of his bedroom door.

*   *   *

Why did I ever get married? thought Hubert as he buried his face in his pillows. Suffocating, demanding women! This rout would be a disaster. She was overworking the servants. Biggs was in a shaky condition with that ball in his chest. He would die. And it would be Mary's fault. And so he would tell her. And with that comforting thought, he fell asleep.

When he awoke, it was already dark. The sound of music filtered up the stairs and he sat up in alarm and, lighting the candle, peered at his watch. Ten o'clock! Why had no one wakened him?

Then he remembered the insane quarrel of the afternoon. He wondered if they had both been mad. He rang for his valet.

'Tell me, Mr. Jones,' he said silkily. 'Why was I not aroused? Am I not to greet my own guests?'

'Her ladyship gave strict instructions that you were not to be disturbed on account of you having the headache,' said his valet nervously, scurrying to lay out his evening clothes.

'She did, did she?' snapped Hubert, all his irrational hatred returning. 'No, lay out my dress uniform. I shall not look like a crow this evening.'

A bare half hour later, he joined his wife at the top of the first floor stairs leading to the chain of saloons and took his place beside her. The first of the guests were only just beginning to arrive, but he felt his fury mounting.

Mary, who had tried to make amends to him by respecting his headache, took one look at his icy face and her heart sank.

'What is the matter?' she whispered.

'Matter?' he hissed. 'You did not intend me to come to this rout, madam. A shabby trick!'

'But I gave the servants orders to leave you asleep,' whispered Mary savagely. 'I think you are drunk or mad or both.'

'By God! You shall suffer for this insolence,' he whispered viciously, just as the Duchess of Pellicombe ascended the stairs.

'Dear Lady Mary and Lord Hubert,' she cried. 'Such a delightful idea. Isn't it delightful?'

'No, it's not,' snapped Hubert. 'I wish the curst flat evening were over.'

'Oh dear,' wailed the Duchess, hastening off on her husband's arm. 'What on earth happened to the motto, "Manners maketh the man"?'

'Control yourself,' hissed Mary to Hubert as the Duchess moved away.

He opened his mouth to make a reply, and then he saw Lady Clarissa coming towards him up the stairs on the arm of Lord Peregrine. Clarissa had surpassed herself. Her burnished hair gleamed like fire, and her green eyes sparkled like the magnificent collar of emeralds round her neck. In fact, at first glance, it looked as if Lady Clarissa were wearing the emeralds and nothing else. Her dress of the finest silk was in a creamy skin color and dampened to mold her body. Lord Peregrine had painted his face to disguise his bruises.

To Mary's surprise, he greeted both of them jovially, despite the fact that Hubert was smiling intimately into Clarissa's eyes. Clarissa laughed lightly and murmured to Lord Peregrine. 'You must not take our dear Hubert so seriously, Perry. Once a rake—always a rake. It is only naive little girls who believe in reformed rakes.'

Mary heard the murmur and her heart sank like a stone. She felt pallid and mousey compared to the glittering Clarissa. Her own dress of silver net, which had seemed daringly low in the privacy of the bedroom, now seemed the height of governess propriety.

Hubert had not yet learned one of the most difficult lessons of marriage—that you cannot give love and affection just when you feel like it. He had spent a long and energetic lovemaking with Mary and for the moment he did not desire her. He therefore felt trapped, and the hurt in her large gray eyes intensified the feeling. He longed to flirt with all the girls in the room and then see the dawn come up through the bow window at White's in St. James's.

Mary felt bewildered and lost. Her husband had suddenly turned into a hard, elegant and indifferent stranger. He looked heartbreakingly handsome in his uniform, and she noticed how other women looked at him and felt a lump of suffocating hurt in her throat.

This rout had really been to show the world that Lord Hubert and his wife were in love—a love such as fickle society had never known before. Still she hoped that when they danced together, he might warm to her. There was to be dancing and cards.

But no sooner had they joined the other guests than her husband abandoned her for the card room. She numbly conversed with various strange faces, and when the dancing began she found with some trepidation that Major Godwin was her first waltz partner. He plunged into his woes immediately and she could not help putting a sad little hand up to sympathetically caress his cheek.

She immediately realized what she had done and quickly took her hand away, but not before she had caught the malice in Clarissa's green eyes and the speculative look on Lord Peregrine's face.

The Witherspoons seemed to be everywhere, pushing and gossiping. At first, they were snubbed as usual but as Mary watched them, she noticed that they were finally gathering an audience and then many startled looks were being cast in Lucy's direction. The Witherspoons were cheerfully burning Lucy's reputation on the social pyre.

Lucy gradually became aware of the hard stares. She looked desperately around for Freddie but he had taken Mary into the refreshment room and seemed absorbed in conversation.

Lucy had arrived late, hoping to make an entrance. Now it seemed she was destined to prop up the wall, while her husband broadcast his infatuation for a married woman.

Her eyes filled with ready tears of self-pity.

'Like Niobe, all tears,' said a gentle voice at her elbow. Lucy looked up into the calm, austere face of Captain Peter Bennet. He made her a low bow. 'We met in Brussels,' he said. 'Peter Bennet at your service.'

'Oh, of course I remember you,' said Lucy. Her heart-shaped face was animated and her tears dried without leaving any unsightly blotches. 'Like a summer flower after rain,' said Peter almost wonderingly.

'How pretty,' laughed Lucy, her vanity

restored. 'How is it we have not seen you in town?'

'I have been ill,' he said briefly. How could he tell this beautiful little creature of the horrid dreams and nervous exhaustion which had plagued his days and nights after the battle? He was normally a cynical and sophisticated man about town. But he had served in the Peninsular Wars from beginning to end, and then had survived the hell of Waterloo. Normally he would have found Lucy vapid and silly and his code of honor would not have allowed him to flirt with a married woman. But in his present state of mind, he would probably have fallen in love with the first pretty girl he saw at the rout. With the luck of the bewitched Titania, the first person he saw had to be Lucy Godwin and, like the fairy queen, he did not even notice the asses ears.

He gazed into her eyes and Lucy exclaimed, 'You should not look so, Mr. Bennet! People will talk.'

'Let them,' he laughed, drawing her into his arms at the sound of the opening strains of the waltz. 'Do you care?'

Lucy's eyes flicked from the gossiping Witherspoons to her husband in the refreshment room with Mary. 'No,' she said breathlessly, feeling the hard grasp of his arm at her waist. 'No, not a bit.'

Mary emerged from the refreshment room

on Major Godwin's arm, just as her husband came out of the card room at the opposite side of the saloon where the dancing was being held.

Their eyes locked and held and one would have said their glances swore at each other. Clarissa floated past him and he caught her arm and said something in her ear. She threw back her head and laughed, her green eyes sliding towards Mary, holding a world of mockery. Hubert had not said anything about Mary at all, he had merely paid Clarissa a light compliment. But Clarissa meant Mary to be hurt and hurt she was. Hubert was being eaten alive with jealousy. He did not recognize the emotion that was tearing him apart. He only knew that everything was dreadfully wrong and that somehow it was all Mary's fault.

From then on the evening did become a nightmare for Mary. Her eyes kept blurring with tears as she danced and laughed and sparkled as best she could, while the tall figure of her husband in his scarlet regimentals seemed to haunt her as he flirted outrageously with, not only Clarissa, but half the ladies in the ballroom.

At the third waltz, she found herself in Major Godwin's arms. 'She won't look at me,' he mumbled. 'Peter Bennet of all people. Fine soldier and a good captain. I must speak to him!'

'So far he has done nothing wrong,' said

Mary gently.

'I wish I were dead,' he said gloomily, treading on her toes. 'Ah, you wince in pain. You know how I am feeling!'

'I am wincing because you are treading on my slippers,' Mary pointed out reasonably. The Major gave her a hurt look. What a child he is, thought Mary.

When the dance came to an end, she began to walk about with him until her next partner should claim her.

Suddenly there was a loud commotion at the top of the stairs. The ballroom fell silent and all eyes turned upwards. Guests crowded to the doors of the refreshment and card rooms to see what was amiss.

Biggs, who had been stationed at the top of the red carpeted stairs to announce the guests, came staggering forward. His face was deathly pale. His hand was pressed to his chest. He staggered painfully halfway down the steps and clutched onto the bannisters. Several of the guests rushed forward, but Biggs suddenly made a superhuman effort and hauled himself to his feet and stared down at the shocked faces of the guests.

His eyes dimly sought out Lord Hubert. 'I'm a-going, Cap'n,' he said. 'Remember Vittoria! Remember Salamanca! Those were the days, Cap'n. I don't regret nothing.'

He staggered on the bottom three steps and turned his white face to the painted ceiling.

'Come on boys!' he yelled suddenly. 'Come along you lazy bleeders or Frenchie'll get you.' His dim boot-button eyes stared down from some dream escarpment across the baking sierras of Spain.

'God save King George,' he cried in a great voice and fell in a crumpled heap on the ballroom floor.

'Dead!' screamed the Duchess of Pellicombe and fainted.

Lord Hubert pushed past the crowd of guests and knelt down on one knee by the side of his old comrade at arms. His hard, bright eyes lighted on his wife who was standing only a few inches from him. She was sobbing uncontrollably. Major Godwin was cradling her in his arms and murmuring soothing things into her curls.

Hubert's distress manifested itself in an all-consuming burst of fury.

'You silly bitch!' he yelled at Mary. 'This is your doing and may God forgive you. You've worked the man to death!'

There was an indrawn hiss of almost shocked enjoyment. The death of a butler, although beautifully staged, was as nothing compared to the delicious sight of the handsome Lord Hubert, 'Beau' Challenge, publicly humiliating his wife.

Peter Bennet gently untangled himself from Lucy Godwin's arms and knelt on the other side of the butler. He thumbed open the butler's eye and then put his head to Biggs' massive chest.

'He's dead all right,' said Peter cheerfully. 'Dead drunk!'

CHAPTER SEVEN

The Challenge rout was discussed for days afterwards—but not in the way that Mary had hoped. The party, which was to demonstrate her husband's love for her to all the Polite World, had ended in showing them that he heartily detested her.

Lord Hubert did not know how to apologize. It was a wife's place to forgive her husband, after all. But no sooner had he tried to take her in his arms after the last guest had left and tell her soothingly that Biggs should be pensioned off, than she had beat at his chest with her fists and called him a monster of ingratitude.

Biggs was the one who had apologized most heartily to both master and mistress, who both readily forgave him but would not forgive each other, Mary feeling she had nothing to forgive and Hubert not wishing to believe that he had.

He took himself off to his beloved Hammonds and Mary did not see him for three whole weeks. When he returned, he promptly set about escorting Clarissa, while

140

Lord Peregrine smouldered in the background. Mary felt her heart would break, but Major Godwin at least was always there to take her about and comfort her.

The Witherspoons avidly watched the members of the quadrille. Their gossip about Lucy had been a great success and they were anxious to supply more. They were to be frequently seen either in Mary's company or in Lucy's, and gradually their malicious gossip that Mary was having an affair with Major Godwin and that Lucy was having an affair with Peter Bennet began to be believed.

Peter Bennet was the first to hear the gossip. He had escorted Lucy to a turtle breakfast and when he had left her to find refreshments for them, he had overheard two dowagers carefully picking Lucy's character to pieces. His infatuation had fled leaving him feeling foolish and appalled at his behavior.

He was no longer available to help Lucy into her carriage or to stand holding her shawl and fan at the opera. He at last also heard the gossip about Lucy's flight from Brussels, and he could hardly bear to look at her. Lucy, deprived of her last flirt, turned her hurt attention on her husband to find that he had apparently deserted her for Lady Mary Challenge.

Lord Hubert seemed much as he had been in his bachelor days. His clothes were the envy of the club, his graceful, muscular figure graced every ballroom in London. It was just as well, people said, that his little wife had found a flirt for herself.

When they met in their home, they treated each other with the polite formality of strangers, while Biggs looked on with anxious, worried eyes. He felt he had been the cause of the break-up in the marriage but, for the life of him, he could not think what to do about it.

He confided as much to the Highland cook who consoled him not at all by pointing out that it was none of his business, whereupon the much-incensed Biggs had called him a haggis-faced petticoat-wearing dumpling, and nearly got a pot of turtle soup over his head.

Then one late summer morning, the eight members of the Brussels quadrille found themselves face to face again—in a room in Horseguards. Each eagerly asked the other why they had been summoned, and finding that no one knew why, their various hatreds reasserted themselves and they glowered at each other in a laden silence.

The door opened at last and the well known, portly figure of General Brian Deveney rolled in with a pale and silent Captain Harry Black.

The general sat down at the head of a long oaken table and motioned the members of the quadrille to take their places around it.

The general ruffled a sheet of paper and cleared his throat. 'You will all recognize

Captain Harry Black,' he began. 'He called at the residence of Clarissa, Lady Thorbury in Brussels. Explain, Captain Black.'

Captain Black wetted his lips and looked nervously around at the party. 'I called at Lady Thorbury's,' he said in a low voice. 'I was to inform Colonel Challenge that we had orders to march. I had a portfolio with me. In it were papers and maps showing the strength of our allied troops, and the placing of the various regiments, particularly near Quatre Bras.

'Lady Thorbury begged me to join them for an after-dinner drink. When I returned to staff headquarters, I left the portfolio in the care of the adjutant. During the battle of Quatre Bras, it was discovered that the portfolio contained nothing but blank sheets of papers. For a while it was assumed that a traitor had stolen them from staff headquarters.

'But,' interrupted the General, 'after a rigorous investigation, headed by none other than His Grace, the Duke of Wellington, it was discovered the papers were removed from the portfolio at your house, Lady Thorbury.'

'Madness!' said Clarissa, her eyes flashing. 'Just because I asked Captain Black to stay for a drink does not make me a traitor.'

'I agree,' said Lucy Godwin surprisingly. 'I am sure it was not Lady Clarissa. But there are some people who would do anything for power and money. Blackmailers!' She stared straight at the Witherspoons.

'Ho, indeed,' snarled Mr. Witherspoon. 'And what about young wives who run away and leave their husbands to die on the battlefield?'

'Freddie didn't die, but that piece of malicious gossip just did,' raged Lucy.

'I think of a spy as one of the *quiet* ones,' said Clarissa lazily, looking pointedly at Mary.

The General held up his hands for silence.

'These pointless accusations are not getting us anywhere,' he said. 'I want each of you during the next week to write down everything you remember about that evening from the moment Captain Black arrived. I shall not detain you any longer—with the exception of you, Colonel Challenge—a word with you in private, I beg.'

The party filed from the room and then hesitated on the steps outside. The Witherspoons went home to rehearse this latest gem of gossip. Lucy looked at Major Godwin in a furious way and insisted on going home alone. Major Godwin escorted Mary. Clarissa looked curiously at Peregrine. 'Here's a coil,' she murmured. 'Who do you think did it, Perry?'

'The General himself,' said Peregrine with a great bark of laughter. Clarissa giggled. 'Of course, you must be right. But now we have to remember all sorts of dreary things. You shall help me write them, won't you darling?'

'After,' he said.

'After what?'

'After this.'

'Perry! In the street. I declare you are becoming as wild as Hubert.'

'Don't mention his name to me. What's your game, Clarissa? You say you are playing him along to revenge me, but it seems to me as if you're enjoying yourself a bit too much.'

'Pooh!' said Clarissa. 'I am a good actress. Come, if you tease me you shall not have your Before.'

*   *   *

Lord Hubert Challenge left Horseguards an hour later in a thoughtful mood. He had no clue as to the identity of the traitor. He only knew it was not himself. It could not be Mary. Freddie would never betray his country. But Lucy Godwin was greedy and silly. The Witherspoons would do anything for social power whether in this country or in France. Clarissa might do it to discover a new thrill. But Lord Peregrine was too cowardly, too much the John Bull in an unappetizingly brutish way.

On his return home, he paced through the spacious, fragrant rooms of his house, looking for his wife but she had not yet returned. He sat down and tried to think clearly. He had to admit he was driving her into the arms of Freddie Godwin and he did not quite know why. He looked back on their quarrel and wondered if he had run mad. He had always been so sure of himself, so ruthless in attaining his aims. He had married to keep Hammonds in the family. He had married for money. He had not dreamed for a minute that the shy, countrified girl he had wed would turn into a woman with a tempestuous range of moods. He suddenly knew that he wanted her in his arms again, so badly it made him feel quite ill.

He wondered again what she thought of him. Her new vivacity had dimmed and her face had resumed some of its old madonna-mask, the eyes wary and guarded.

He had imagined a wife as being someone grateful, admiring and compliant who would be ready to accept his love and affection at precisely the time he felt like giving them, and at all other times would sit somewhere unobtrusively with her sewing, until he was ready to notice her again—not racket around the town with a married army officer.

He realized that if he wanted her he would have to go about courting her, and the idea made him angry. One should not have to court one's own wife.

Nonetheless, as the day wore on and she did not return, he changed into his evening clothes, dressing with elaborate care and sent orders to the kitchen to prepare an especially good dinner.

MacGregor, the Highland cook, drove Biggs

into a fury by pointing out smugly that his best French dishes would be just the thing to restore tranquility to the household. But Biggs was a devoted servant, so he swallowed his spleen and lined his army of servants up for inspection and gave them their orders. They were to be quiet and unobtrusive. James, the first footman, was to order flowers for the dining room and for my lady's bedroom. Then Biggs hit on a brainwave. A band of musicians should be hired to play soft romantic music in the hall—there was some Viennese lot who were fashionable at the moment.

His heart quailed however when he took a tray of decanters in to the Green Saloon early in the evening. Her ladyship had not returned, and his lordship was looking about as romantic as a thunderstorm.

As he was gloomily descending to the hall, the street door opened and Mary came in. She looked white and tired, as indeed she was. She was tired of listening to Major Godwin's troubles and had snapped at him that all Lucy needed was a good shaking. She loathed the very sight of Clarissa and was sure that Hubert was in love with her. That time of passion, which had meant all the world to her, had been, she was sure, merely a *divertissement* for her sophisticated husband. She had been on the town for long enough to realize that a great proportion of society treated their sex lives in the same way they treated gourmet cooking, something to be savored and enjoyed while someone else did the dirty dishes. One had affairs with anyone other than one's spouse, and never let messy emotions like love spoil the fun.

She looked up and saw the anxious face of Biggs.

'I shall not be dining this evening,' she said quietly. 'I am very tired.'

'Oh, you can't do that, my lady,' said Biggs anxiously. 'His lordship has commanded such excellent dishes and MacGregor would break his heart, my lady, if they were to go to waste.'

'My lord is dining at home!' exclaimed Mary in surprise.

'Yes, my lady,' said Biggs, 'and he has already changed for dinner and awaits you in the Green Saloon.'

Mary gave a sigh. 'Very well, Biggs. Tell my lord I shall join him shortly.'

Biggs made her such a low bow that his bristling head nearly touched his shoes and then rushed off to tell MacGregor of his splendid diplomacy in getting my lady to take dinner.

Hubert was seated by a small fire in the saloon and looked up briefly as his wife entered the room. She was wearing a lingerie gown of pale green muslin trimmed with little gold oak leaves. Her hair which had grown longer was piled on top of her head in an artless cluster of curls. A chain of gold oak leaves had been threaded through her curls. She looked remarkably pretty and very young.

She dropped a curtsy to her husband, who was once again staring at the fire, and sat down in a high backed chair opposite him.

Had she arrived some two hours earlier, he would have swept her into his arms. But he had grown angry at being kept waiting, forgetting that he had not dined at home for some time. As if remembering his obligations to an unwanted guest, he rose to his feet and poured her a small glass of wine, placed it on a table beside her, and resumed his brooding over the fire, the flames playing on the stern plains of his face and sparking fire from the diamond pin in his stock and the diamond rings on his long forgers.

'Was it not a strange meeting at Horseguards?' asked Mary timidly at last.

'Very,' he said coldly. 'I am sure you have already mulled over the matter with Major Freddie Godwin.'

'As you no doubt have with Clarissa.'

'We will leave Clarissa's name out of this, if you please.'

'Of course,' sneered Mary nastily.

'I merely do not wish to bicker this evening.'

'Dinner is served,' announced Biggs.

Lord Hubert offered his arm to his wife. Mary put the tips of her fingers on his sleeve as if she were afraid of contracting some contagious disease. Biggs' boot-button eyes darted from one angry face to the other and with a little sigh he made a smart rightabout turn and led the way downstairs.

As soon as his master and mistress were seated at the table, Biggs realized it was going to be a bad evening. Both my lord and my lady were usually in the habit of noticing and appreciating any special effort on the part of the servants. But the splendor of the dining table, with its beautifully polished silver and crystal, its elaborate flower decorations, its tempting dishes, went unnoticed by the glacial pair.

Remove after remove was carried back to the kitchens untouched, as the couple sipped their wine and brooded on each other's iniquities.

How long this state of affairs would have lasted is hard to say. But the cook, MacGregor, finally could not stand the insults to his art any longer. He erupted into the dining room, an angry barbaric figure in his military kilt, his red beard glistening with rage.

'It iss mair than the flesh and bluid can stand,' he roared, advancing on Lord Hubert. 'Sassenachs wass always the same. Ice water in your veins. My verra soul went into those dishes, my lady, my lord. Do you care? Och, it takes the heart out of a body.'

With that he tore off his chef's cap and flung it on the floor and then collapsed into a chair, hugging his large body and rocking backwards and forwards, wailing, 'Ochone, ochone!' in a high keening voice.

Mary sat in shocked silence. Biggs was wringing his hands. Lord Hubert raised his quizzing glass and studied his cook in startled amazement.

'If you will stop that damned Gaelic wailing, MacGregor,' he said icily, 'and try to explain slowly and carefully in English the reason for this disgraceful behavior.'

'It iss yourselves,' moaned the cook, too distressed to guard his tongue or remember his place. 'We are sad to see my lord and my lady at odds so we work and slave to bring ye together again. I am inspired. Neffer haff I cooked as I haff cooked this night. Och, what's the use!'

He resumed his keening, while his master slowly lowered his quizzing glass.

Out in the hallway, the small six-piece orchestra hired for the occasion burst into the opening chords of 'Oh, Nights of Passion.'

'Stop that damned caterwauling, MacGregor,' snapped Lord Hubert, 'and bring all the dishes back and you, Biggs, bring all the servants here! Bustle about man!'

MacGregor stopped his wailing and fled from the room. Biggs marched after him, while the orchestra played on.

'Oh, Hubert,' said Mary, the tears standing out in her large eyes. 'I feel we are behaving very badly.'

One by one the servants marched into the room and stood against the wall. MacGregor and the kitchen staff followed, bearing the rejected dishes.

Lord Hubert stood up while they all hung their heads and waited for the outburst. 'Now,' he said, 'I and my lady are indeed touched by your efforts to please us. We have indeed been remiss in not noticing your attentions.' He smiled down the long length of the table at Mary, and her heart gave a painful lurch. 'You must not be so depressed by our marital rows, must they, my love?'

Mary smiled back at him weakly.

'So, my lady wife,' said Hubert, stretching out his hand, 'if you will come and sit by me, I think we shall celebrate our loyal servants' devotion. All of you, pull your chairs to the table, and we shall sample the MacGregor's art.'

*　　　*　　　*

The Duchess of Pellicombe's carriage swung over the cobbles of St. James's Square in front of the Challenge mansion. The dining room curtains were drawn back, affording the Duchess an excellent view of Lord and Lady Challenge entertaining their servants to dinner.

'Good gracious!' she cried, her eyes almost popping out of her head. 'Do but look. The

Challenges dining with their servants!'

The Duke leaned across her and stared from the carriage window at the brightly lit tableau.

'Challenge must have turned radical,' he grunted, settling back in his seat. 'That sort of thing breeds anarchy. I shall speak to that young man very sternly.'

*   *   *

Mary watched her husband's animated face as he refought old battles with his servants. The wine was flowing freely, his face was flushed and alive. He had never looked so handsome. He had never before looked so much a stranger.

'Right you are, Captain—I mean my lord,' cried Biggs, excited by the tales of battle. The butler turned his twinkling gaze on Mary. 'Saved my life, many's the time, 'is lordship did. 'Member when Frenchie was levelling a pistol at me and I was saying me prayers. His lordship creeps up behind Frenchie and slices 'is 'ead clean off. How we laughed! That poor Frenchie's 'ead was a-rollin' on the ground with such a look of surprise on 'is face as you never did see, my lady.'

Mary repressed a shudder and gave a weak laugh. Then she felt the pressure of her husband's hand on her knee under the table.

How could she possibly go to bed this night

153

with this bloodthirsty stranger? She moved her knee away from his hand and he snapped his head round and stared down at her, as if finding some subaltern guilty of dereliction of duty.

Then a faint, wicked gleam began to burn at the back of his eyes. 'Come, my love,' he said, throwing down his napkin. 'It is time we retired.'

Mary blushed painfully, and all the servants got to their feet and stood waiting.

'Three cheers for the Captain!' shouted Biggs. There was nothing else to do but to take her husband's arm and leave the room as the resounding *huzzas* split the quiet air of St. James's.

Her bedroom looked dark and mysterious and sinister to Mary's frightened eyes. It was lit by only one small candle placed beside the bed and the dark, saturnine face of her husband seemed to glow above the darkness of his body.

'No, I *can't*,' said Mary helplessly. 'Not tonight, Hubert. I am not feeling at all the thing. Hubert! Why are you taking off your clothes. You are not attending to me. Leave me *alone*. I am perfectly capable of undressing myself! Oh, my gown! You monster! You have ripped my gown! Oh, *no*! Oh, Hubert. Oh, *darling . . .*'

*   *   *

The watch announced to the interested that it was two o'clock and a fine night.

In the upstairs bedchamber of the Challenge mansion, Lord Hubert initiated his bride further into the mysteries of the marriage bed. At one point, Mary surfaced from a sea of passion to protest faintly, 'The position is awkward and monstrous undignified, my lord.' But her husband, his face strangely drawn and tense in the light of the guttering candle, merely looked down at her and said, 'I love you, Mary,' and she closed her eyes, grasped tightly onto the muscles of his shoulders, and forgot everything else.

The watchman announced the three o'clock in a hoarse stentorian voice, as if peeved at his lack of audience.

Mary turned sleepily in bed and looked at her husband. He was wide awake, staring up at the bed canopy.

'*Clarissa*,' he said. 'Clarissa, by all that's holy.'

He hurtled from the bed and began to put on his clothes with the same rapidity with which he had taken them off.

Mary struggled out of the mists of sleep and fatigue and sat up in bed clutching the crumpled sheets to her naked breasts.

Her husband was emanating a quivering air of excitement, like a war horse scenting battle.

'If you go to Clarissa at this hour,' said Mary

155

in a low, even voice, 'our marriage is finished.'

Lord Hubert swung around, staring at her as if not quite hearing or seeing her. 'Fustian,' he said vaguely. 'I shall return shortly.'

Mary sank back against the pillows, as wave after wave of misery and shock engulfed her. After such a night of love, he had left her to go to Clarissa. He was a degenerate, an unfeeling monster. And she loved him.

She turned her face into the pillows and cried until a pale dawn began to streak the sky.

CHAPTER EIGHT

A thin drizzle was falling as a hired hack drew up outside Major Freddie Godwin's house. The Godwins lived in that network of small streets at the back of Park Lane. The houses were the same as those of the grand squares and of Park Lane itself, except that they were much smaller and had the appearance of being squeezed together to make room for as many desirable gentlemen's residences as possible. Even the tiny shops considered it the height of vulgarity to display all their wares in their windows, so that you had to guess that it was, say, the grocer's by one basket of plovers' eggs in the window, or the baker's by two varnished wooden loaves.

Into this stagnant pool of gentility stepped

Lady Mary Challenge at six o'clock in the morning.

She paid off the hack after the driver had deposited her trunks on the pavement, and brushed the straw from the skirt of her carriage dress before mounting the worn steps of the Godwins' residence. Assuming—quite rightly—that the bell probably did not work, she rapped loudly with the tarnished brass knocker and waited.

There was a long silence and then the slow, shuffling sound of footsteps.

A sleepy, cross butler opened the door a crack and stared disapprovingly at the heavily veiled figure of Lady Mary.

His eye swiveled 'round the crack, looking for an attendant maid and, finding none, began to close the door again.

Mary put her small half boot in the crack and, made courageous by misery, said in a loud voice, 'I am come to see your master. Rouse him immediately or it will be the worse for you.'

The butler opened the door two inches. He wanted to send this unescorted young miss to the rightabout but something in her voice gave him pause.

'Master's asleep,' he said sulkily. ' 'Tis dawn and respectable people are abed.'

'Fetch Major Godwin immediately,' said Mary grimly.

Reluctantly the butler opened the door wide

157

and led Mary into a small dingy saloon on the ground floor.

After some time, Mary heard him mount the stairs and then the shrill sounds of an altercation. She could not make out the words but she could recognize Lucy's voice. Then she heard a heavy tread of the stairs and Major Godwin walked in, looking as if he had hurriedly scrambled into his clothes—as indeed he had.

'Oh, *Freddie*,' said Mary brokenly. 'Take me home.'

'Indeed, yes,' said Freddie equably, as if being roused from his bed at dawn by young matrons was an everyday occurence. 'Delighted to be of service. I shall have my carriage brought round directly and you shall be home in St. James's Square in a few minutes.'

'Not *there*,' wailed Mary. 'I mean *home*. My parents' home.'

'Is anything wrong with Hubert?' asked Freddie.

'Everything's wrong with Hubert,' said Mary bursting into tears. 'He-he d-doesn't l-love me. He's gone to Clarissa. At three o'clock this morning. He l-left our b-bed and w-went to Clarissa.'

'Here. Steady on. There must be some reasonable explanation.'

'What?' demanded Mary through a mist of tears.

Major Godwin thought long and hard, twisting his sideburns in his large fingers. But it was too unusual and painful an exercise for him, so he at last said dismally, 'Don't know.'

And Mary, who had somehow hoped that he would come up with some dazzling explanation, threw herself into his arms and cried in earnest.

'There, there,' said Freddie helplessly, putting back her veil and trying to dry her eyes with his pocket handkerchief. But she only cried harder than ever, so he merely hugged her close, trying to comfort her as he would a hurt child.

'Philanderer!' cried Lucy from the doorway. 'What, pray, is the meaning of this?'

'I'm going off with Mary,' said Major Godwin, made stupid by embarrassment.

'*What?*' screamed Lucy. 'Explain yourself, sir, this instant.'

'Oh, I say,' began the Major awkwardly, about to make his usual humble apology. But in that moment, he saw the full blaze of jealousy in his wife's eyes and recognized it for what it was. He was overcome by a mad desire to hurt Lucy as badly as she had hurt him, so he turned his attention to Mary and stroked her back with a large, comforting hand. He then looked coldly at his furious wife over Mary's head.

'We're going off together,' he said, savoring every word.

Lucy glared at him, and then her natural vanity reasserted itself and she laughed, 'Stop teasing, Freddie. You would never leave me in a hundred years and you know it. I don't believe a word of it. And just to show you, I am going back to bed and I am going to leave you to your silly schoolboyish games.'

She gave a malicious little titter and flounced out of the room.

'I'll escort you,' said Freddie heavily. 'Come, Mary. Dry your eyes. It will do us good to leave London for a bit. The servant shall bring you some tea while I fetch my trunk.'

A bare half hour later, Lucy Godwin leapt from bed at the sound of her husband's carriage being brought 'round to the front of the house. With unbelieving eyes, she watched the servants strapping her husband's trunk up at the back, along with Lady Mary Challenge's luggage. She threw up the window and leaned out.

'Freddie!' she screamed. But the broad back of her husband disappeared into the darkness of the carriage and a footman slammed the door behind him. The coachman on the box cracked his whip, and the carriage swayed off down the narrow street.

Lucy's beautiful mouth folded into a thin line. Lord Hubert Challenge should hear of this.

*   *   *

Mrs. Witherspoon was awakened by a commotion below her bedroom window. Ever curious, she opened the window and leaned out, her great bosoms spilling over the sill.

A small trunk had rolled from the back of a traveling carriage and had broken open. Fine silks and satins were spilling out into the greasy mud of the street. Mrs. Witherspoon settled her elbows on the sill and prepared herself to thoroughly enjoy every bit of someone else's misfortune.

The carriage door opened and a heavily veiled young lady descended followed by a large young man. Mrs. Witherspoon recognized the young man as Major Godwin. Then the young lady, who was instructing a groom on the refastening of her damaged trunk, threw back her veil. Mrs. Witherspoon drew in her breath in a hiss of excitement. Mary Challenge! That high and mighty, hoity-toity Mary Challenge with none other than Freddie Godwin! Beau Brummell himself would listen to such a marvelous piece of gossip. And as for Lord Hubert who looked at the Witherspoons as if they had crawled out from under a rock—how he would smart.

She watched avidly until the couple re-entered the carriage and moved off.

She was about to leave the window when she saw another familiar figure. She leaned out again. Viscount Lord Peregrine St. James was

161

standing outside his house a little way down the street, staring after the departing carriage. Then he swung about and rushed indoors. Mrs. Witherspoon waited. Two minutes later, his horse was brought round and Lord Peregrine swung himself up into the saddle and galloped off in the direction the carriage had taken.

Lord Hubert Challenge should hear of this—for a price.

*   *   *

'I've told you and *told* you,' said Lady Clarissa. 'Now I wish you would go away.'

How could I ever have loved this monster? thought Clarissa angrily. Lord Hubert had dragged her from her bed in the small hours of the morning and had questioned her over and over again about that wretched dinner party in Brussels. He was sure he remembered Perry sliding some papers behind the clock. 'What of it?' Clarissa had yawned. She always stuffed letters and things behind the clock in the dining room. Perry probably thought they were love letters and had taken them out to look at them. Hubert must know by now how jealous Perry was.

'I am well aware of Perry's jealousy,' said Hubert grimly. 'But I am not leaving until you think a little harder. Did Perry ever say or do anything that might lead you to believe that he

162

would turn traitor?'

'Oh, anything to be rid of you,' groaned Clarissa. 'Very well. He rather admired Napoleon, but Perry is a Whig so that is nothing strange. I would not become affianced to a man who would betray his country.'

'Why do you want to marry Lord Peregrine?' asked Hubert, stopping his pacing of her bedroom and coming to stand over her.

'Because you married that silly widgeon,' snapped Clarissa, too tired to speak less than the truth.

'But you still mean to go through with it?'

'Oh, yes, yes, yes. He amuses me. He's a brute. I like brutes. But I no longer like you, Hubert. You are merely boorish and unpleasant and my head aches so. Go and ask Perry. That would surely have been a more intelligent thing to do than bursting into my bedroom and supplying my servants with gossip.'

'I thought to find him here,' said Hubert.

'And having not found him, why did you not leave immediately?'

'Because I want to confront him with some evidence. Now think again, Clarissa. We all left the dining room when Captain Black arrived . . .'

Clarissa sighed loudly. The drizzle had thickened into a heavy rain which pattered mournfully against the windows.

'Well . . .' Clarissa was beginning, when

there was a timid scratching at the door and a maid entered, her head down and eyes averted. One never knew, after all, what one would find in the Lady Clarissa's bedroom.

'An it please my lady,' she whispered. 'Mrs. Witherspoon is below demanding an audience. Mrs. Witherspoon says as how she has urgent news of Lord St. James.'

'Tell the old baggage to take her gossip out into the kennel where it belongs . . .' began Clarissa wrathfully, but Lord Hubert was already at the door.

'I shall see her,' he said to the maid, ignoring Clarissa's horrified cry of, 'How dare you give that tattle tongue more food for gossip, Hubert!'

He ran lightly down the stairs and entered Clarissa's drawing room.

Mrs. Witherspoon dropped him a magnificent curtsy, the feathers on her turban quivering with anticipation.

'It is a shocking miserable day, is it not?' she said leering up at him as she rose from her curtsy.

'You did not come calling at this hour of the morning to exchange pleasantries on the weather. Out with it,' said Hubert grimly.

Mrs. Witherspoon smiled at him coyly, not in the least put out by his angry manner. 'I could not find you at home,' she said, 'and as it was a matter of some urgency, I thought Lady Clarissa might know your whereabouts.'

'Now you found me,' snapped Hubert. 'But since your news is about Lord Peregrine, what concern is it of mine?'

'Ah, that would be telling,' smirked Mrs. Witherspoon. 'I would like it understood that if I do your lordship a favor I expect one in return.'

'How much?'

'La, it ain't *money*,' giggled Mrs. Witherspoon. 'Me and my husband only ask for a little social kindness in return, if your lordship takes my meaning.'

Hubert stared at her in baffled rage. Then he said in measured tones, 'It is believed that Lord Peregrine may be a traitor to his country, ma'am. You will give me any information you have, or by this night every fashionable drawing room in London will be calling you his collaborator.'

Mrs. Witherspoon shrank back in her chair away from the blazing anger in his eyes. 'Well, I don't want to be the one to pass along bad news,' she said sulkily. 'But your wife left at around six and a half hours of the morning with Major Godwin.'

Hubert looked down at her with an expression she could not fathom.

'And,' he suddenly said quietly, looming over her, 'you also mentioned Lord Peregrine—or had you forgotten.'

Mrs. Witherspoon looked up into his eyes and what she now saw there terrified the wits

165

out of her. She shakily stood up, edging sideways away from him and began to babble. 'Lord Perry started riding after them. That's all, my lord. Please let me go. It's late I am for my dressmaker. That's all I know.'

'Go then,' said Hubert, looking at her with disgust. 'But keep that silly tattle-tale mouth of yours closed, madam, or it will be the worse for you. I cannot call you out, more's the pity, but there is always your husband.'

Mrs. Witherspoon gave a horrified squawk and, gathering up her voluminous skirts, fled the room.

Hubert barked out an order to one of Clarissa's footmen to fetch his racing curricle.

Returning to the drawing room Hubert sat down heavily and buried his head in his hands as wave after wave of hot, burning jealousy swept over him. He wanted to find Mary and take her in his arms and tell her he loved her; he wanted to choke the life out of her. Gradually his hot brain began to clear and he had a sudden and vivid memory of leaving Mary in the small hours of the morning to see Clarissa. He had expected her to know what he was thinking. She had obviously thought he had fled from her arms to Clarissa's and God only knew he had given her enough reason to think so. She was probably returning to her parents and had persuaded Freddie to take her. Freddie was not the man to elope with anyone else's wife. He roused himself and went to wait for his curricle.

*   *   *

Lucy Godwin went in search of Lord Challenge at St. James's, only to be told by a footman that he could be found at Lady Thorbury's.

As Lord Challenge was pulling on his York tan driving gloves and pacing up and down impatiently on the doorstep, he felt an imperative tug on his arm. Lucy Godwin looked up at him, her eyes bright with tears.

'Freddie has eloped with Mary,' wailed Lucy.

'Fustian,' snapped Lord Hubert. 'He is merely escorting her to her parents.'

'But he *told* me so,' sobbed Lucy whose self pity had made Freddie's brief words appear to have been a full scale rejection. 'He threw back his head and laughed at me and said he'd always loved Mary, and that he was leaving with her.'

'Out of my way,' said Hubert coldly. 'I am going to follow them in any case.'

'Take me with you!' screamed Lucy, hanging onto his arm.

'I am driving my curricle,' said Hubert impatiently. 'You are not dressed for an open carriage in this weather.'

'I will not melt,' said Lucy with surprising vigor. 'I insist on going.'

'Don't complain then,' he rejoined curtly.

He sprang up into the curricle and a footman helped Lucy mount by way of the wheel. She wrapped herself in rugs and tried to ignore the driving rain which was making a sorry wreck of her new bonnet. After fifteen minutes of swaying and jolting, she whispered a complaint that she felt sick.

Lord Hubert Challenge paid her not the slightest heed whatsoever.

*   *   *

A watery sunlight was beginning to bathe the English fields as Mary and Major Freddie Godwin jolted along side by side, each silently immured in their own thoughts. Freddie was cursing himself for his weakness, but he could not help regretting not telling Lucy the true state of affairs. The poor little love had been so terribly jealous.

He had admired Mary as being a sensible woman, but now he began to feel that this situation was somehow all her fault and longed to return to Lucy to be bullied and humiliated once more. For her part, Mary was beginning to feel foolish. Perhaps she should have stayed until Hubert came home and asked him the meaning of his strange behavior. As the miles rolled under the carriage wheels, and London faded in the distance, she could only remember Hubert's voice as he said he loved her.

Freddie rapped on the roof of the carriage with his cane. 'Pull up at the next posting house, John,' he called to the coachman. He leaned back against the squabs. 'We will both feel better when we have had something to eat,' he explained gently.

Mary answered him with a miserable little nod. The sun was beginning to beat on the carriage roof making it uncomfortably warm inside. A hot tear ran down her cheek and splashed on the skirt of her gown. Love was not what she had imagined it would be.

She had dreamt of a tranquil, affectionate relationship. Not this burning, unsettling emotion that made you believe the worst of the one you loved. She suddenly could not bear it any longer. She did not care if Freddie was angry with her. She simply had to go back.

She turned to speak to her companion when the carriage lurched to a sudden halt, nearly throwing them on the floor.

'What the devil . . .' began Freddie, jerking down the carriage window and thrusting his head out.

Then in front of Mary's horrified eyes a pistol butt came down on the top of his head, and he slowly toppled forward through the window. Then the carriage door was jerked open and Lord Peregrine St. James stood there with a more unpleasant expression than usual on his heavy face.

He pulled Mary out onto the grass beside the road and, as she kicked and screamed, called on some unseen assistant for help. Rough hands wrenched off her bonnet and turned her face down on the grass, while her wrists and ankles were firmly tied. Then she was twisted over and a wad of gun cotton was stuffed in her mouth and she was gagged with a handkerchief.

Mary rolled over and stared wildly upwards. Lord Peregrine had three uncouth helpers; coarse, brutal looking men. The coachman and the groom were lying trussed up beside the road, and Freddie was lying on the grass where he had fallen, blood streaming from an ugly gash on his head.

All was suddenly very quiet. The only sounds were of the birds chirping in the hedgerows and the faint barking of a dog several fields away. The black clouds of the morning had rolled away, leaving the day hot and sunny, smelling of the grasses and flowers of the countryside, the pastoral scene somehow intensifying the nightmare.

Lord Peregrine stooped down and picked Mary up into his arms. She averted her eyes from his leering face.

Still he did not speak. He carried her to another traveling carriage which had been swung across the road and threw her in on the floor among the straw. One of his helpers took the reins and the other two jumped up on the back strap.

Lord Peregrine prodded Mary lazily with his boot as she rolled backwards and forwards helplessly on the floor as the carriage sprang forward and lurched and swayed as it headed down the road towards its destination.

Mary closed her eyes tightly to blot out Lord Peregrine's face and tried to think. What would Hubert think if he did not find her at home? Perhaps he would not care. All her jealousy for Clarissa came pouring back and her anger gave her courage.

One thing was sure. Hubert would never find her. She would need to lie very still and watch and wait for a chance of escape. But secretly she felt this was the end. She looked up at Lord Peregrine and read her death warrant in his eyes.

The carriage rolled on and on. Once it slowed in the narrow streets of a market town and the shaggy head of a yokel peered in at the carriage window, his eyes popping out of his head at the sight of a gagged and bound young lady lying on the carriage floor. Mary stared up at him, her eyes dilated, pleading for help. Then Lord Peregrine shouted, 'We'll never get to Dover at this pace!' and the carriage rolled on. No cry of alarm was raised. Mary had never felt more frightened or more alone.

At long last, they stopped to change horses. With a slow smile, Lord Peregrine threw a blanket over Mary and all hopes she had of rescue faded to one little dot of light. *He has abducted you before*, a little voice of hope nagged in her brain, *and Hubert rescued you then*. But that small gleam of hope was almost agonizing. Better to prepare her mind for death.

The blanket was removed and the headlong flight continued. Night fell and a pale sliver of moon lurched and swayed along beside the carriage. Lord Peregrine fell asleep, leaving Mary to stare up at the moving sky. Where was he taking her? And if he wanted to kill her, why take her so far?

At last, as a red dawn barred the sky, Mary fell asleep and did not awake when the carriage stopped to change the horses again.

She awoke to the sound of the carriage wheels rumbling over cobbles and then she thought she could smell the sea. Suddenly, from overhead came the high, thin scream of a seagull.

The carriage door was opened by one of the ruffians who jerked his thumb at Mary. 'Best put her in a sack me lord so's we can take 'er on board without fuss.'

Lord Peregrine nodded. 'Fair enough, Jim. Slide it over her legs. Stay *still*, damn you.' For Mary had begun to feebly kick out with her bound feet.

Then she lay still and let them bundle her up in the sack. When she was carried from the carriage, she planned to wriggle up and kick to attract attention. She felt herself being heaved up onto Jim's back. She waited until he had stumbled a few steps with her and then she began to kick and wriggle in earnest. 'Seize 'er feet, man,' Jim whispered to one of the ruffians.

'What have you got there?' called a jolly voice and Mary tried to wriggle harder, although her feet were now being held tight.

'As prime a porker as you ever did see,' yelled Jim cheerfully.

'I like 'em with a bit of life in 'em,' answered the jolly voice. 'Move once more and I'll knock you unconscious, you plaguey woman,' muttered Jim, and Mary ceased her struggles.

Soon from the creaking of wood and the hiss of the wind, Mary judged she was being carried aboard a vessel. She was bumped and banged ruthlessly down a short flight of stairs. There was a grunting and wheezing as Jim dumped his load and searched for a key. Then she was picked up and, a short minute later, dumped onto the floor. The stifling sack was jerked from her head and then her body. Then the gag was taken from her mouth by an ungentle hand, and the ropes that bound her wrists and ankles were cut. She groaned aloud as the circulation began to return to her hands and feet, aimed a feeble punch at Jim, and fainted dead away.

'That'll keep 'er quiet till 'is lordship's ready for 'er,' muttered Jim. He went out and carefully locked the cabin door behind him.

CHAPTER NINE

Lucy Godwin had almost forgotten her misery over her husband's unfaithfulness. She had never felt so battered, beaten or bruised in her life.

Lord Hubert was driving neck or nothing through the now sunny countryside. She had screamed in protest several times as her ferocious driver had skimmed past a farm vehicle on the road with barely an inch to spare. The members of the Four-In-Hand Club would have cheered. Lucy begged in vain for Lord Hubert to stop the nightmarish pace.

The colors of the summer fields streamed past her terrified eyes. Then the horses surged over the crown of the road and Lucy screamed in earnest as she spied a carriage blocking the roadway, and the still figures of three men lying in the ditch. At one moment it seemed as if they surely must crash headlong into the stationary carriage. But the next, Lord Hubert had skimmed past it, grazing his nearside wheel.

He slowed his horses to a trot and then reined them in. His frightened groom ran to their heads and, without even looking at Lucy, Lord Hubert jumped lightly down and strode back along the muddy road which was steaming in the hot sun.

He walked round the carriage and looked down at the body of Major Freddie Godwin. 'Help us!' cried a voice, and he turned and saw the coachman and groom struggling with their bonds. He quickly untied them and returned to Freddie, kneeling down beside him and examining the gash on his head.

'It wor that Lord Peregrine,' gasped the coachman. 'He hits master on the head with the blunt of his pistol, while his servants hold me and Johnnie up at pistol point.'

A faint scream from behind him brought Lord Hubert's head round with a snap. 'No, he is not dead—yet,' he told the trembling Lucy. 'I hear the sound of a stream nearby. You fellows, soak handkerchiefs and place them on Major Godwin's head and then convey him gently to the nearest inn and send for a physician.'

Freddie groaned and opened his eyes. 'Mary,' he said weakly.

'What of her?' said Hubert in a low, tense voice. 'What has he done with her?'

'Taken her off,' said Freddie weakly. 'I don't know where. They—they tied her up. I came out of my swoon for long enough to hear one of them say they had a long ways to go.'

'I must go after them,' said Hubert quietly. 'Lucy is here and your servants will attend to you. Has no carriage passed here since?'

'I don't know,' sighed Freddie. 'I've been dead to the world. Mary was going home to her parents, Hubert. Wasn't going away with me, old fellow. Wanted an escort. I . . . I wanted to make Lucy jealous. Do you hear that, Lucy?' But Lucy had gone to fetch water.

Hubert pressed his hand in reply, and strode back towards his carriage. He could only hope and pray that he could keep a track of Lord Peregrine.

*　　*　　*

At first it was easy since Lord Peregrine had been traveling at a hectic enough pace to draw attention, but then at a large crossroads the trail went cold, and there was nothing he could do but scour the surrounding towns and villages.

He was weary, and hungry and mad with worry and concern when he finally stopped in the market town of Little Beddington. There had been a fair that day and knots of people were still standing around the town square. At first they seemed alarmed by his vehement questions, until one farmer vouchsafed that one of his men had a 'powerful funny story' about looking in the window of some lord's carriage and seeing a young lady tied up on the floor; but no one had paid much attention seeing as how the fellow was 'touched in his upperworks.' The yokel who had seen Mary

176

was at last found and slowly and painfully told his story.

'Where were they bound for?' cried Hubert. 'Think! For God's sake *think*.'

The yokel became sulky and hung his head and said he didn't know, until his ox-like gaze fastened on the piece of gold that Lord Hubert was holding under his nose.

'Duvver!' he cried, all of a sudden anxious to please.

'Dover?' asked Hubert. 'Are you sure?'

The yokel smiled, lolling his great head from side to side.

'Duvver, it wor.'

'Don't 'ee believe our Clem,' said the farmer soothingly.

'I'll have to,' said Hubert grimly. 'Pray God he is right!'

*   *   *

Peter Bennet was a very disturbed and worried young man. He sat in a corner, unobserved, at the Duchess of Pellicombe's breakfast, and listened to the ebb and flow of gossip around him.

The presence of the Witherspoons had been a shock. They had arrived with Mr. Cyril Trimmer, that young man being more pomaded and padded and corsetted and wasp-waisted than any other person in the room. Peter had mildly asked the Duchess the reason

177

for the Witherspoons' invitation; to which that good lady had replied somewhat incoherently that England was heading for a revolution, and one could no longer be so high in the instep. Even the Challenges were entertaining their servants to dinner!

But it soon became all too evident that the Witherspoons' social value was in their fund of gossip and they were soon surrounded by a crowd of listeners three deep. Mrs. Witherspoon had happily forgotten Lord Hubert's threats as soon as she was safely back at her husband's side. Mr. Witherspoon had promptly sent a note to the Duke of Pellicombe hinting at all kinds of social outrages—hence the coveted invitation.

Peter listened to the gossip with growing alarm. Mary Challenge had fled with Major Godwin. Lord Hubert had been found at Clarissa's house. Lord Peregrine was a Bonapartiste spy. Only the famous Beau Brummell appeared indifferent to this fascinating news. It had amused him to bring little Lady Mary into fashion. But he had not thought of her for some time, and was supremely uninterested in the others.

A newcomer arrived with the information that Lord Hubert's servants had said that Lady Marry had gone to stay with her parents and that his lordship and Mrs. Godwin had gone to join them.

Peter still had a bad conscience over his

flirtation with Lucy Godwin. All of London society knew that the Godwins were becoming increasingly estranged, and Peter blamed himself for the breach in their marriage.

Whether Lord Peregrine were a traitor or not troubled him not in the slightest, but he felt that the least he could do was to try to get the Major and his wife together again.

He suddenly decided to ride down to Mary's parents and see what he could do. Peter was surprisingly unworldly at times for such a sophisticated man-about-town.

He accordingly returned to his lodgings to change and rode out from London in the pale, primrose light of late afternoon.

He had traveled several miles through the countryside when he came to a small town with an attractive-looking posting house. He was debating whether or not to stop for a glass of ale before continuing on his way, when, to his surprise, he heard his name being called. He looked up and there was the pretty face of Lucy Godwin looking down at him from a casement window.

He sat very still, his mind seduced by the romantic picture they made—the pretty girl leaning out of the window among the rambling roses under the golden thatch of the inn, the swimming lazy golden light of evening, the stillness of the countryside and the young cavalier, seated on his horse, looking up. Then he shook his head to banish such mawkish

179

thoughts and sprang down lightly from his horse and entered the inn. Lucy met him at the foot of the stairs, her beautiful eyes brimful with excitement. She poured out the tale of their adventures leaving Peter with only one point to grasp hold of in all the outpourings. Major Godwin had been hurt.

'Take me to your husband immediately,' he said more abruptly than he had intended.

Lucy smiled and shrugged. 'Oh, if you please, but Freddie's all right now. The doctor says he has a thick skull.' And with that she went off into a trill of laughter.

Nonetheless she ushered Peter into a low bedchamber where the Major sat in a chair beside the window.

Until Peter's arrival, the Major had been cursing himself for his stupidity. Lucy had at first crooned over him and nursed him tenderly. It had been wonderful. 'Am I not better than that drab, Mary Challenge?' she had kept asking jealously. At last the tenderhearted Major had held her in his arms and had told her that Mary had been upset over something, and that he had merely been escorting her home and that he loved only Lucy. Lucy's affection had ceased from that moment, and she had spent more time in her room than in his.

He looked up as Peter Bennet entered the room. He looked from Peter's handsome face to Lucy's flushed and excited one, and his face hardened.

'Peter came looking for me,' giggled Lucy who had managed to elicit the information that Peter had been on his way to the Tyres to see them.

'That is not the case at all,' said Peter heavily. 'Pray leave me with your husband, Mrs. Godwin.'

Lucy started to protest and then backed away from the expression in Peter Bennet's eyes. He closed the door behind her and turned to the Major. He hardly knew how to begin.

Major Godwin continued to stare at him and at last, with a sigh, Peter drew up a chair and sat down.

'You may have been aware that at one time I nursed a certain *tendre* for your wife,' began Peter awkwardly.

'Yes,' said the Major in a flat voice.

'I came in search of you to offer you my sincerest apologies for my behavior,' said Peter quietly. 'I was, I believe, still shocked from the Battle of Waterloo and Mrs. Godwin seemed like an angel to me. If I have done anything to cause you distress, I am bitterly sorry for my conduct. Is there any way in which I can remedy the situation?'

He sat with his head bowed, his face taut with embarrassment and distress.

The Major's large heart was touched. 'No, Captain Bennet,' he said quietly. 'The damage

181

was done before you appeared. I have hung around like a fool watching Lucy flirt with one gallant after another. When she met you, I feared her heart was engaged . . . but she has no heart. I appreciate what it cost you to come here. But there is nothing anyone can do for me.'

Peter's sensitive soul writhed under the other man's distress. He abruptly changed the subject. 'What is this villainy of Lord Peregrine? What is all this about a meeting at Horseguards?'

'The Witherspoons I suppose,' asked the Major heavily and Peter nodded.

'Then I may as well tell you.' He told Peter about the missing papers. 'But that does not make Peregrine the villain,' he pointed out at last. 'He is mad with jealousy over Lady Clarissa's obvious interest in Lord Hubert.'

'So you think that may be why he abducted Lady Mary?'

'It could be. Good God . . . someone must inform the authorities. Are you returning to town?'

Peter nodded. 'I shall go straight to Horseguards, never fear. But surely, Lord Hubert would send one of his servants?'

The Major shook his large head. 'That one would not stop or think until he found Peregrine. I informed the local magistrate of the abduction but not of the matter of treachery.'

Peter rose and tried to find some words of comfort before he left. He could not bring himself to present his compliments to Lucy. He made the Major a stiff bow and turned towards the door.

'I say—Major Godwin,' he said with his hand on the latch.

'Yes?'

'I would beat her, you know—beat her soundly.' And with that he was gone.

A few minutes later, Lucy bounced into the room and made a *moue* of disappointment. 'Oh, has Peter gone?'

She ran to the window. '*Cooee*, Peter!' She turned a laughing face to her husband before turning back to the window again. 'Such a handsome young man! Peter! I shall see you when I return to London and you shall tell me all the *on-dits*.'

Lucy was leaning far out of the window, looking as if she might topple out at any minute.

Her husband surveyed her with a red mist of anger beginning to blur his eyes. He rose from his chair and walked over to where she stood with her back to him. He jerked her back with a rough hand and sitting down on the bed, he pulled her across his knee and proceeded to administer a good hiding, deaf to her screams.

Every inn servant listened to the screams with great satisfaction. They hoped the trollopy Major's wife was getting her just desserts. For Lucy had flirted with almost every customer in the inn.

His rage did not last long. He buried his head in his hands as she slumped to the floor at his knees. It was all so incredibly hopeless.

Then to his amazement, he felt a pair of soft arms winding round his neck and a soft voice saying, 'Oh, Freddie, I do love you so.'

Major Godwin slowly took his hand away from his face and stared down into his wife's shining eyes. Of all things, he thought. His brutal handling of Lucy had won him the response he had dreamed of. It was a strange sort of love but if it made his wife look at him like that . . . well . . . He pulled her roughly into his arms and began to make love to her with a well-simulated savagery.

*   *   *

Peter Bennet rode slowly through the tranquil blue light of the evening. He thought of the Godwin's marriage with fastidious distaste. He thought of old battles, and once again his ears reeled with the thud of the cannonade and the bark of shot. The tranquil evening fled before his frightened eyes as the noise of battle became more deafening and he saw ghostly, mutilated bodies lying beside the road. He stumbled from his horse and sat beside the road, covering his head with his arms, trying to ward off the nightmare terrors of war. It was his worst attack yet.

And then he heard the bells of evensong.

Faintly, they sounded through the roar of battle and then gradually they came to his ears, sweet and clear.

He raised his head.

He only saw now the quiet fields and, some distance away, the gray walls of an Anglican monastery. The pale scents of the summer evening came to his nostrils. Up in the violet sky, the first star of evening shone bravely down.

With a calm, single-minded purpose, he remounted and rode steadily across the fields towards the monastery, towards home.

And that is how Society lost one of its most elegant ornaments, and how the gentlemen of Horseguards heard nothing of Lord Peregrine's villainy that day.

CHAPTER TEN

The wind sighed and moaned in the shrouds of *The Avenger* as the trim sloop swung at anchor in Dover harbor.

Mary had pounded on the door of the cabin, and screamed until her lungs were hoarse, but the only sounds that came to her ears were the occasional high-pitched cry of a gull and the whining of the wind. Night had fallen. The small cabin was furnished with a table and two chairs and a low berth in one corner. A brass lamp swung dizzily from the low ceiling. Then, above the wind, she heard the sound of voices on the quay.

'It's a powerful deal of yelling she's doing,' said a rough voice. And then quite distinctly came the smooth reply of Lord Peregrine. 'I've told you all, my sister is mad and to pay no heed. It's a sad business, but mayhap she will fare better in a sunnier clime. Come, my friends. If I had not volunteered to remove her from these shores, our relatives would have had her in Bedlam.'

Then came the sound of steps on the gangplank, then above Mary's head, and finally descending the ladder to the cabin. As he opened the door, Mary made one desperate bid for freedom, flinging herself on Lord Peregrine and clawing at his face with her nails. He gave her a violent shove and she fell back against the berth.

He lit the lamp, and then came and stood over her, dabbing at the scratches on his face with a handkerchief. 'Now Lady Mary Challenge,' he sneered. 'I suppose you wonder why I have brought you here.'

'Revenge,' gasped Mary. 'You would be revenged on Hubert because he gave you the thrashing you deserve.'

'Correct,' he smiled, 'but I must also leave the country. It would only be a matter of time before those fools at Horseguards found out that it was I who stole the papers from Captain Black.'

'You are a traitor,' said Mary flatly.

'I am a loyal supporter of Napoleon. He will escape again, mark my words, and then I will come to power. England will be under French rule and I shall be regent.'

'You're mad,' said Mary in a voice that broke on a sob. 'Why are you taking me with you?'

'I'm not,' he said, moving closer to her while the lamp above them swung in a dizzying arc. 'Your first guess was correct. I want revenge on that oaf, Hubert. I shall have you first, then I shall kill you and leave your remains in a sack on the quay for dear Lord Hubert Challenge to find. I cannot set sail because of this accursed storm, but it cannot last forever.'

'What of Clarissa?' begged Mary desperately.

'That one will console herself with someone else soon enough—probably with your husband.'

'He would not have her,' cried Mary, steadying herself as the boat made a wild, bucking lurch. 'He married me!'

'And regretted it ever since,' sneered Lord Peregrine. 'Clarissa was too unfaithful a type of woman for him. He wanted to gain his money by marrying a respectable little mouse.'

'Then he will not care if I am dead,' pointed

out Mary, grimly trying to keep him talking.

'You forget, you are his possession like his horse or his dog. I shall have revenge enough.'

Both stared at each other in silence, Lord Peregrine in greedy cruelty, Mary wide-eyed, almost numb with fatigue and shock.

Above and below them pounded the tumult of the storm. The boat plunged and reared, riding and tossing and straining at anchor like a nervous thoroughbred. The gale shrieked and hissed and moaned in the shrouds. A flicker of apprehension appeared in Lord Peregrine's eyes. Perhaps he had been foolish to allow his crew to spend such a night ashore.

Something broke loose on the deck above and set up a wild, rhythmic thudding.

There was another great heave and lurch and both staggered trying to gain their balance. Then with a great crack, *The Avenger* struck against the side of another boat. Lord Peregrine started in alarm and Mary began to hope again that there might be some way of escape. But Lord Peregrine's greed for revenge was too strong. He moved closer to Mary and put a large, beefy hand on her neck. 'Plead for mercy, Mary,' he laughed. 'Plead for mercy and I might let you live!'

Mary stared up into his gross brutal face and all the fight left her. 'Hubert,' she said with a weary sigh and closed her eyes. She heard his excited labored breathing and waited for the feel of that awful, brutal mouth against

188

her own.

There came a loud report and the sound of splintering wood. The cabin door flew open and Lord Peregrine abruptly released Mary and stared in alarm.

Lord Hubert Challenge loomed on the threshold. He held a smoking pistol in one hand and a drawn sword in the other. The door with its lock shattered from his shot swung wildly on its hinges as the boat plunged and heaved in the storm.

'Leave the cabin, Mary,' shouted Hubert. 'Get behind me!'

Lord Peregrine stood swaying, his face black with rage, his hands fumbling to fasten his breeches. His eyes never left Hubert's face as Mary, holding her hands to her face, scurried behind her husband and stood at the foot of the companionway.

'Your sword, Lord St. James,' said Hubert in a voice like ice.

A gleam lit up Lord Peregrine's eyes. He would normally be no match for Hubert's swordsmanship, but in this reeling, plunging cabin he might have a chance.

Mary sat on the bottom step of the companionway as the rain lashed down on her and buried her head in her hands and prayed.

The two men began to thrust and lunge and parry, ducking their heads to avoid the swinging oil lamp which threw grotesque shadows on the cabin walls. Lord Peregrine fought with a mad courage born of desperation and once he slipped under Hubert's guard and his sword point pinked him on the shoulder. The sight of Hubert's blood drove Peregrine to further efforts. He thrust his sword point up through the glass of the lamp and plunged the cabin into darkness. He could just make out the doorway of the cabin as a sort of lighter blackness.

He heard a noise over to the left of him and made a dash for the doorway, throwing his great bulk directly ahead to freedom.

He ran full headlong into the point of Lord Hubert's sword.

Lord Hubert pulled his sword clear and backed out of the cabin, fumbling behind him to find Mary and then pulling her to him in a strong grasp.

Lord Peregrine's heavy, dying body reeled blindly around the darkness of the cabin like some great moth looking for the light. At last there was the sound of a heavy fall, and then silence.

'Come, Mary,' said Hubert urgently. 'The boat has been holed. The water's coming in already.'

They struggled up the companionway and up onto the deck, gasping as sheets of icy rain struck their faces. They ran along the plunging, reeling deck to the gangplank only to find it had been wrenched from its moorings and lay shattered like matchwood below them on the quay.

The air was full of rain and screaming wind and the smash and rattle of ships being battered at anchor. Great masts danced and dipped and bowed before the storm like some demented forest.

Hubert cupped his hands to his mouth. 'John!' he yelled to his groom, who was standing guard on the quay. There came a faint answering shout above the storm.

'John, catch my lady. She's coming over.' The white face of the groom suddenly appeared directly below them on the quay.

'Mary,' said Hubert urgently. 'I'm going to throw you over. John will catch you. Do you understand?'

'Yes,' said Mary, dazed, and battered and buffeted. Would this ordeal never end?

He picked her up lightly in his arms. 'Ready below?' he called, and, at John's answering call, he tossed her over.

Mary was expertly caught by John and placed on her feet. She stared upwards, seeing the black bulk of her husband leaping down towards her from the ship.

'She's a-going, my lord,' said the groom, jerking his thumb in the direction of *The Avenger*. 'She's been holed.'

'Let her sink,' said Hubert indifferently.

He huddled Mary close to him and began to run. 'I have to find us rooms and shelter,' he shouted above the storm. 'It won't be very long now.'

It was well that Lord Hubert was known at that famous hostelry, The Blue Anchor, or the landlord would certainly not have unbarred his doors on such a night.

Mary was hustled into a warm bedchamber, sleepily clutching hold of her husband as he removed her sodden clothes. He shook her gently.

'Did I arrive in time, Mary?' And Mary could only dumbly nod, weak tears of relief beginning to pour down her face.

'I must go and report this to the authorities,' he said quietly. 'Sleep, Mary. You need no longer be afraid. Peregrine is dead.'

But Mary had already fallen asleep in his arms. He picked her gently up and carried her to the bed, stroking her hair back from her white face.

'Thank God she is alive,' he murmured. 'I will never raise my voice to her again.'

CHAPTER ELEVEN

'I said we are going to the Duchess of Pellicombe's ball and let that be an end of it,' shouted Lord Hubert Challenge at his wife, Mary. 'Those damned, gossiping, tattling Witherspoons must be put a stop to. They have been having a tremendous time while we

192

have been gone, planting and sowing all kinds of disgraceful rumors. You have had a full fortnight to recover from your ordeal, madam, which is more than is granted to any soldier.'

'I am not in your regiment,' snapped Mary, her eyes bright with tears. Men were so boorish, so stupid. How could she ever have believed she loved him. He was as insensitive as an . . . as an . . . as an *ox*. It was too good a piece of imagery to waste.

'You are as insensitive as an ox,' said Lady Mary.

'You shall answer for that piece of impertinence later,' said her husband grimly, winding his military sash round the waist of his red and gold dress uniform.

Mary turned and stared out of the window. She had hardly been able to believe her ears when Biggs had brought her a curt note from her husband, telling her to prepare herself for the Duchess's ball. She had reluctantly arrayed herself in a pretty silver-spangled gown and had sent for the hairdresser to tease her lengthening curls into one of the fashionable Grecian styles. But she could not resist walking along the corridor to her husband's rooms to protest at his accepting the invitation.

She had lain in the Dover inn for a week after her ordeal, feeling nervous and weak and shaken. On the seventh night Hubert had tried to share her bed and she had shrunk away from him with a cry of alarm as Lord

193

Peregrine's brutal features seemed to be suddenly imposed over those of her husband.

He had brought her back to London where she had kept to her rooms, eating her meals from a tray. All her old timidity had returned and she shrank from seeing anyone, even Hubert.

But now her unfeeling husband was dragging her out into the world again.

She maintained a chilly silence all the way to the ball.

The Duchess of Pellicombe greeted them rather nervously. Really! One no longer knew what to expect from the Challenges. Or from anyone, for that matter. Clarissa had arrived with not a thread of mourning on her. The affair of Lord St. James had been hushed up but one *knew*. So many whispers and the Witherspoons appeared to be an endless source of fascinating gossip.

Lady Clarissa was the first guest to welcome the Challenges. She looked magnificent. She had lost weight and used more water than ever to damp her gown, hiding hardly an inch of her superb figure from the interested gaze.

She did not mention Lord Peregrine. It was as if the monster had never existed, thought Mary, hanging rather sulkily onto Hubert's arm. Clarissa rattled and chattered very amusingly and at a great rate, her beautiful face animated.

Hubert was at first all chilly condescension.

194

But at last his eyes began to light up in a smile of appreciation at one of Clarissa's naughtier stories and Mary, unaware that her husband now cordially detested Clarissa but wished to punish his wife, heard him asking Clarissa for the next dance.

As they moved away together, Mary saw one of her former dancing partners approaching and hid behind a pillar. The ballroom was very hot, illuminated as it was with the light of hundreds of wax candles. The windows at the end of the room opened onto a terrace from which steps led down to a pleasant garden.

Mary made her way there and leaned over the balustrade and looked down. The Witherspoons were holding court beside a lily pond. Mrs. Witherspoon's feathered headdress nodded back and forth. There were excited *oohs* and *ahs* from their listeners. Suddenly the music behind Mary ceased, and Mrs. Witherspoon's voice rang out loud and clear, 'I hear Lord Hubert's dancing with Lady Clarissa. That pair have no shame. His poor little wife . . .'

Not stopping to think, consumed by hurt and a burning rage, Mary ran down the stairs to the garden and straight up behind Mrs. Witherspoon who stood facing the pool. Raising one little slippered foot, Mary kicked out with all her might and Mrs. Witherspoon sailed into the lily pond, face down in the water. Mr. Witherspoon turned round and his large ingratiating face with its permanent leer was too much for Mary. Still panting with rage and exertion, she kicked him in his well-stuffed stomach, and he toppled backwards to join his wife.

Lord Hubert, who had stood amazed on the terrace with Clarissa, watching the antics of his wife, ran down into the garden and swept Mary into his arms and gave her a kiss that left her breathless.

'Oh, my joy,' he laughed. 'I could not have done better myself. Mary, Mary, when you are cold with me, you make me behave so badly. What will you do with me?'

Mary clutched hold of him. 'Take me home, Hubert.'

He looked down at her blushing face and kissed her very tenderly. 'Home it is,' he said, leading her gently from the garden.

The Witherspoons sat in the lily pond and saw their social ruin in the disdainful faces looking down at them. Fickle society admired Mary's spirit, and now stood united against the upstart Witherspoons and their malicious gossip.

'*Laugh!*' said Mr. Witherspoon, poking his wife under the water. 'Laugh as hard as you can.'

Mrs. Witherspoon stared at her husband as if he had gone mad, but she dutifully began to laugh as hard as she could, joined by Mr.

Witherspoon who bellowed with mirth as hard as *he* could.

The guests, who had been turning away, turned back and stared at them in amazement. Even mock laughter is infectious, and soon one joined in and then another until the Witherspoons were surrounded by a circle of guests howling with mirth.

One intoxicated young man became so carried away that he hurled himself into the water with a tremendous splash. Soon all sorts of people were leaping into the pool and tipsily congratulating the Witherspoons on their party spirit.

Mr. Witherspoon exchanged a covert wink with his wife. They were still in society—for the time being anyway.

The Duchess of Pellicombe stared into her garden as if she couldn't believe her eyes. What a rowdy disgrace! What had happened to all the ladies and gentlemen? She closed her eyes firmly and turned around and then, opening them again, marched into the ballroom. If she did not watch the disgraceful goings-on, perhaps they would simply go away.

But the Duke had already seen the pool party. 'You know,' he confided to his wife, 'there are some curst rum touches around society these days.'

And the much-plagued Duchess of Pellicombe burst into tears.

Lord Hubert's carriage wound its way through the country lanes at a leisurely pace. Mary sat beside her husband with her hands tucked into her muff, for the sunny day was unusually cold for early autumn, and tried to fight down an attack of nerves. She was finally going to see Hammonds, and felt as nervous as if she were going to meet a rival. The wooded countryside grew more open and rolling and a stiff breeze sent a small hail of beech nuts rattling into the carriage roof. A field of grass stretched out to her left, rolling and turning in the glittering yellow light of the setting sun.

A pheasant, startled by the rumbling of the carriage wheels, rocketed up clumsily and disappeared over the hedge. A flock of starlings whirled and chattered against the lemon yellow sky.

Her husband was asleep, his body moving easily on the seat to the lurching and swaying of the carriage. Mary pressed her hand against her stomach. She was sure she was pregnant. Would her son—for she was sure to have a son—be worthy of this country estate she was at last going to see? Would she?

The carriage slowed and turned and swung through an ancient pair of moss-covered gates. Hammonds!

Her husband awoke and smiled at her sleepily. 'Nearly there,' he yawned. 'Biggs has

198

been there all day, marshalling his troops so we should have a comfortable night.'

Mary smiled at him weakly, feeling increasingly nervous. Soon the carriage left the brown and gold fields of stubble behind and began to roll through wooded parkland where deer flitted silently through the trees, as fabulous and romantic in the flood of late golden light as unicorns. Everything seemed to be a rich blaze of green and gold as if a Gobelin tapestry had come to life.

'Hammonds!' said Hubert with a deep note of satisfaction in his voice.

The carriage had left the woods and was bowling through open parkland.

Hammonds nestled in the foot of a small fold in the landscape—or rather it crouched.

It was one of the nastiest houses Mary had ever seen. If a house could be said to grumble, then it certainly did. Heavy ivy hung over the windows, giving the ludicrous effect of heavy lowered brows. It was a jumble of roofs and fantastically twisted chimneys. It had been built in Tudor times out of a singularly repellent yellow brick. Some ancestor had tacked on a wing in a florid Gothic style, which sprang away from the main building at an awkward angle.

It will be charming inside, thought Mary, fighting down a feeling of disappointment.

Biggs stood on the worn steps, his large face looking strained and creased. But summoning up his best manner, he clicked his heels smartly together and said, 'Welcome my lord, m'lady.'

He turned about and led the way into a low dark hall where a great fire sent acrid puffs of smoke up to the already blackened beams. The whole place smelled of damp and dry rot and, despite the fire, had an all-pervading chill.

'Begging your lordship's parding,' said Biggs, clearing his throat. 'But was your lordship intending to make a long stay of it?'

Hubert smiled warmly round the decay of his family home.

'For the rest of our lives,' he said.

'Blimey.'

'I beg your pardon, Biggs.'

'I said I was going to show you to your room, my lord.'

'I can find my own way, Biggs,' said Hubert, throwing his butler a suspicious look. 'Come, Mary.'

Mary obediently took his arm and allowed him to lead her up the stairs, which creaked and groaned in protest.

He led her down a low corridor on the second floor and down a small flight of steps to a low door at the end. He flung it open. 'Our bedroom, my love,' he said.

A small fire crackled on the hearth, hissing and spitting and sending vicious little puffs of smoke into the freezing air. One of the servants had left the small windows wide open, no doubt in an effort to dispel the smoke. A vast great four poster bed dominated the room. Its dingy, threadbare hangings moved in the breeze from the open windows. A smoke-blackened tapestry covered most of one wall. It depicted a deer being disembowelled in splendid clarity. There were no carpets on the floor. An enormous wardrobe which looked as if it could house a whole army of ghosts loomed from the gathering shadows.

'What do you think of your home, Mary,' said Hubert, standing with his back to her and looking out of the window.

'It's *awful*,' said Mary in a choked voice. 'And you married me to save this . . . this . . . crumbling, smelly heap of decay.'

Hubert swung around. 'You must be mad,' he said slowly. 'Of course, it is hard for you to appreciate a *real* family home when one takes into account that prissy, prim, soulless box of a place you were brought up in.'

'My home,' grated Mary, 'is well-run and isn't in any danger of falling down with dry rot and decay. This place stinks, my lord. It stinks of bad cess and all sorts of nasty, nasty things.'

'Your mind is a cesspool,' said her husband in a cold, level voice. 'You see life accordingly. I have never been so insulted in all my life . . .'

'Oh, Hubert,' sighed Mary, 'I am not insulting you. I am insulting this run-down hovel.'

'Then don't live in it, madam,' he said, his eyes hard and glittering in his flushed face. 'I am going out riding and when I return, I expect you to have removed your presence from my home.'

He stalked from the room and Mary ran furiously after him. 'You can't expect me to travel all the way back to London when I have just arrived,' she shouted to his retreating back.

'Go to London—go to hell for all I care,' said Lord Hubert, descending the staircase. 'Just get your unwanted presence out of my home!'

'Oh, Gawd,' said Biggs, retreating hurriedly to the kitchen. 'They're at it again.'

He fortified himself with a bumper of brandy in the pantry and then made his way up the stairs, scratched on the door of his mistress's bedroom and walked in. Mary was sitting, dry-eyed in a chair by the window. She turned hard eyes on the butler.

'Ah, Biggs. I shall shortly be leaving for London. Please have the travelling carriage brought round and send Juneaux to me.'

Biggs rubbed his hands distractedly through his powdered hair. 'My lady,' he began awkwardly. 'It's not my place to say so but it's a bit sudden like and them 'orses—horses—is tired.'

'My lord commands it, Biggs,' said Mary with a dreary smile. 'I offended his delicate sensibilities by pointing out that his ancestral home is a slum.'

'And so it is,' said Biggs eagerly. 'I am talking out of hand, my lady, but think what that place in St. James's looked like before you changed it. There's a lovely little saloon on the ground floor, not half bad, and the fire draws sweet. If you was to let me lead you there, my lady, and have a cup of tea, you might see things different.'

'Oh, very well,' sighed Mary, anxious to postpone the long journey back to London.

The saloon was hardly lovely, but it was warm and cheerful and someone had placed a large copper bowl of beech leaves and chrysanthemums, a flower Mary had not seen before. The walls were covered in faded panels of yellow silk and the furniture was comfortable, if shabby.

Biggs set the tea table beside her and then went over to an old settle in the corner. He lifted up the lid and came back bearing a roll of gold brocade.

'See here, my lady. This here would look ever so fine as curtains. There's so much we could do.'

He rolled out the cloth and held it up to his bosom, staring at her anxiously. The fold of rich gold cloth fell around his feet and Mary giggled, despite her misery. 'You look very well, Biggs,' she laughed. 'Just like the Marquise Elvira.'

Biggs's small eyes twinkled and then he cocked his head on one side, 'Master's home,' he said. Mary stiffened, her face going hard.

'Compringmise,' whispered Biggs urgently. 'That's what my Ma who had book-learning used to say. It don't hurt to tell a bit of a lie. Tell 'is nibs you like the dump.'

Mary hesitated, torn between taking Biggs's advice and giving him a stern set-down for his over-familiarity.

The door opened and her husband walked in, drawing off his gloves. Mary rushed into his arms crying, 'I am so sorry, Hubert. I was tired, that is all. I think it is my condition . . .'

'You mean . . .' Hubert's face changed from stern anger to radiant pleasure like lightning. 'Biggs you may leave us—although what you are doing parading round in cloth of gold looking like . . . Hey, I think I know who you look like. You look exactly like that Marqu . . .?'

'Kiss me, Hubert,' said Mary.

Biggs tactfully retreated, closing the door behind him and trailing the swathes of gold cloth to the kitchen.

'My lord and my lady are reconciled,' he said dreamily to the cook, MacGregor.

MacGregor sniffed and rattled the pots and pans violently.

'It'll not last a day,' he said gloomily.

But it did!

And for much, much longer than that . . .

We hope you have enjoyed this Large Print book. Other Chivers Press or Thorndike Press Large Print books are available at your library or directly from the publishers.

For more information about current and forthcoming titles, please call or write, without obligation, to:

Chivers Press Limited
Windsor Bridge Road
Bath BA2 3AX
England
Tel. (01225) 335336

OR

Thorndike Press
295 Kennedy Memorial Drive
Waterville
Maine 04901
USA

All our Large Print titles are designed for easy reading, and all our books are made to last.